This book should be returned to any ~~~ n of the
Lancashire County Library ~

eyhound George

LANCASHIRE COUNTY LIBRARY

3011813122254 3

Greyhound George

Tony Cleaver

Winchester, UK
Washington, USA

First published by Roundfire Books, 2014
Roundfire Books is an imprint of John Hunt Publishing Ltd., Laurel House, Station Approach,
Alresford, Hants, SO24 9JH, UK
office1@jhpbooks.net
www.johnhuntpublishing.com
www.roundfire-books.com

For distributor details and how to order please visit the 'Ordering' section on our website.

Text copyright: Tony Cleaver 2013

ISBN: 978 1 78279 721 0

All rights reserved. Except for brief quotations in critical articles or reviews, no part of this
book may be reproduced in any manner without prior written permission from the publishers.

The rights of Tony Cleaver as author have been asserted in accordance with the Copyright,
Designs and Patents Act 1988.

A CIP catalogue record for this book is available from the British Library.

Design: Lee Nash

Printed and bound by CPI Group (UK) Ltd, Croydon, CR0 4YY

LANCASHIRE COUNTY LIBRARY	
3011813122254 3	
Askews & Holts	13-Mar-2015
AF GEN	£8.99
NFL	

We operate a distinctive and ethical publishing philosophy in all
areas of our business, from our global network of authors to
production and worldwide distribution.

Inspired by the Retired Greyhound Trust

Chapter 1

As was his custom in the mornings, George Potts staggered blearily out of bed and into the bathroom. Under automatic pilot, he would not really wake up until thoroughly immersed in the shower. On the weekends he allowed himself the luxury of wrapping himself in a towel and, returning to the bedroom, blundering about slowly cogitating over what he was going to do and thus what to wear for the coming day.

This Saturday he observed his wife Annabel, still motionless, covered up in her bed. Although he guessed she was already awake, he surmised she was feigning sleep and waiting for him to leave the bedroom before she stirred. That being the case, George slowed everything down and shuffled around even more absent-mindedly before trying to find the appropriate garments to greet the day. He got as far as a pair of briefs before pausing in front of the full-length mirror and there deciding to take stock of what sort of man this was peering back out at him.

Receding hairline – so far receded in fact that the main passageway was clear right over to the back. It was as if someone had passed the lawnmower through the hallway, leaving only a sliver of carpet on either side, and that was greying.

Eyes – a sunken, lifeless, muddy blue. No sparkle evident.

Teeth? George pulled back his lips to reveal a reasonable set in front but there were several gaps at the back, he knew.

Looking down he saw several gangling, spidery, somewhat uncoordinated limbs, devoid of anything resembling muscle.

There was a developing paunch. Not too noticeable until he turned sideways. Evidence of an overly sedentary existence.

Let's face it – not the most attractive physique. Perhaps his wife was right to resist the urge to turn round and concede she was in fact sharing this room, this house, this marriage with such a decidedly unattractive male.

OK, George, he said to himself. *Maybe you are a pretty repulsive specimen of the human race. So,* he asked, *is there anything I've got going for me?*

He couldn't think of anything. He wasn't wealthy. He had a dead-end job. He was hopeless around the house – if anything broke he couldn't fix it. The workings of both cars and computers were a mystery to him. Wasn't there *anything* he was good for?

He was kind to animals. He supposed that was something. He liked all dumb creatures. He even liked insects and point blank refused to kill spiders, even though they scared the wits out of Annabel. Come to think of it, that was perhaps the reason why he wouldn't kill them.

Annabel! What a name she'd chosen for herself. He'd got to know her when she was just ordinary Ann. That might have been the reason he married her. Yes it was. Nothing flamboyant. Nothing complicated or pretentious. But as the years passed, she started calling herself Annabel. Very fancy. He supposed it was to compensate for his inability to provide the upward social mobility she craved.

He looked back in the mirror. He wasn't too bothered at what he saw. He knew that there were lots of fitness freaks that went regularly to work out, lift weights, run and row or cycle for miles on stupid machines that were fixed to the floor. He could never see the sense of that. If he wanted to run or ride a bike or row a boat then he'd go do that and see where that took him; see what sort of scenery would pass him by, not flog himself to death in some sweaty room full of sadistic machines, smug narcissistic athletes going nowhere and closed in by grey, monotonous walls. No, he was happier being unfit, even if his tee-shirt had never clung to his torso like Arnold Schwarzenegger and his trousers flapped like flags around two flagpoles.

Saturday morning. Perhaps he'd go for a walk at the back of the village before breakfast? That implied a jeans and jumper day. Yep, he'd do that. It was a bright, clear, early morning, the birds were still singing and he might see one or two dogs he liked.

George fancied getting a dog, though Annabel wouldn't consider it: a biggish dog, a real animal – not some stupid yapping thing that was overly domesticated and totally unlike its original wolf-like forebears. If he ever did get a dog it would be a big, silent, uncomplicated beast – a loyal, unfussy companion he could share walks with and certainly nothing pedigree, highly strung and paraded around like a fashion accessory.

He'd said something like that once to Annabel but she'd poured scorn on the idea.

"That's just about the limit! Talk about going to the dogs...your whole life has been one long sustained decline and if you get some big, dirty, flea-bitten canine then that will set the seal upon it. If you get a dog that sniffs all around the streets and lifts its leg at every tree and lamppost, I won't know which of the two of you will be worse. I'll not let a dog in this house...and I'm not sure about you either!"

So: no dog then.

But it was a beautiful day in early May with all of the countryside abuzz with activity, so he'd go out and commune with nature while it was still early. He pulled on the appropriate clothes, whistling to himself and wondered how much noise he could make, bumbling about, without making it obvious that he was trying to annoy his partner in life. He banged the door on the way out.

The first few yards of the footpath that led out across the fields was a bit of an obstacle course – lazy dog owners just drove up to the lay-by, parked and pushed their pets over the wooden stile that marked the entrance to the path and let them do their toilet there before returning home again. However, once George had negotiated this minefield he was away across an open field, up to a distant hedgerow that led an undulating route, eventually criss-crossing with other paths that would take him either further away or round and back home.

Twenty minutes of ambling in the sunshine with his mind wandering more than the footpath and suddenly a great, leaping, elastic creature bounded up to say hello. George was shaken out of his reverie but quite pleased to find a doggy friend. It was a greyhound.

"Rosie! Rosie!" A distraught owner was calling the greyhound from some distance away.

George looked down at the animal that was the cause of the disturbance. It was a long-legged bitch that cavorted around him, sandy-coloured, extremely fit and if dogs could grin, this one was doing it.

"Hello, old girl," George called, "you're a happy soul, aren't you!" He held out one arm towards her.

The dog came up to lick his hand, wagging her tail furiously.

"Rosie! Come back here! Bad girl!" The owner came jogging up: a tracksuited young woman, clearly embarrassed that her dog had run away from her.

George turned to look at the tracksuit running towards him. He felt his temperature rising. Tracksuits that fitted like that were a threat to civilisation. They shouldn't be allowed out. It was dark blue with a slim yellow line running around the owner's bust and down her arms and legs just accentuating curves that would make even a statue break out in a hot sweat, and poor George was not made of stone. That tracksuit was definitely illegal; a provocation; a likely challenge to public order.

"I'm very sorry; I've told her not to run up to strangers. You never know how they might react...mind, she does seem to quite like you." The tracksuit stopped swaying and mesmerising George's vision and a smile swam up into his consciousness.

"Er, yes. A lovely girl. Beautiful creature...very friendly." George wasn't quite sure which creature he was referring to but the tracksuit continued smiling.

"Well I'm pleased you say so. I guess Rosie is lucky this time to find a welcome. Thank you so much." The smiling tracksuit extended a confident hand. George shook it. "My name is Carol and I must say that Rosie really does like you. You have a winning way with animals!"

The greyhound was looking up at George, making affectionate sounds and still grinning at him. George, meanwhile, was trying to control his temperature: he felt as if his face had gone several shades of purple. He was wearing a loose-fitting jumper but somehow it still seemed a bit tight around his neck. Inserting a couple of fingers at the top he pulled it down, blowing out through pursed lips like a demented steam train. Realising this must seem an odd response to his highly attractive visitor, George tried to cover it up by making a succession of fizzing and clucking noises that he directed at his canine companion, hoping that it looked as if he was fluent in animal-speak. He guessed not. He reckoned it only succeeded in making him look a complete weirdo.

"Chkk, pssst, hmm, er...I don't know about winning ways. But I do like most animals...I think I do." George blundered shyly and hoped he didn't come across as too moronic and uncoordinated in front of this self-assured, sensual and very fit-looking young filly. He hoped she would soon go galloping off and leave him to his confusion.

Not so lucky. Carol just beamed at him, recognising someone who wanted to withdraw into his shell and determined not to let him.

"Well, Rosie doesn't often run up to people like that. Never to people she doesn't know. Do you work with animals? Are you a vet or something?" She paused and a wicked look came into her eyes. "No...Don't tell me, let me guess – you work in a travelling circus!"

George was shocked. What an outrageous suggestion. Who was this woman?

"No, no," he flustered. "I'm an accountant...for the council...nothing to do with animals, circuses, or vets..."

"You could have fooled me," Carol retorted. "I could have sworn there's some repressed wildness about you somehow. It's in the way you walk. But an accountant? Never would have guessed that. But I'm impressed – I can't get the hang of figures myself. C'mon, Rosie. Bye!"

She turned, grinned back at him and then set off jogging along the footpath the way that George had come. George just stood there, nonplussed, staring after her: the tracksuit swaying away from him into the distance; Rosie the greyhound bouncing alongside her.

What an extraordinary encounter. Now there, disappearing as he watched, was a figure that George couldn't get the hang of – what sort of female was that? And the comments she made – so blunt and forthright. George was still blushing at the thought of them. Where did all that stuff about repressed wildness come from? The way he walked? George always thought of himself as an ungainly, clumsy fellow who was about as wild and untamed as tap water. And if he hadn't started out that way, he certainly was now after twenty odd years of marriage to a carping matriarch. But the tracksuit thought he worked in a travelling circus! George shivered. He resumed his walk, watching himself as he did so, being extremely careful that he gave no indication of lack of control on his part. Wildness? No, that would never do.

Back at the house, breakfast with Annabel was the usual one-sided conversation.

"George, you will have to stay in and wait for the deliveries that are coming this morning. I'm going to be at the hairdressers and I don't know when I'll be back. And keep the neighbour's cat out of the back garden, will you – I don't want it using the rose bed for its toilet. Are you paying attention? Keep it out, do you hear! And do clean up your study for a change – I'm sure it's the most disgusting room in the whole house. Your desk is worse than the council rubbish tip, it really is. Why you can't see that

6

I'll never know. Just try and make it presentable so that when people come round I am not mortified if they catch a glimpse inside..."

George nodded and tried to look attentive. His mind was already some distance away, however, thinking of tracksuits and travelling circuses. He smiled encouragingly to his wife, hoping it looked like he knew what she was talking about. Perhaps she would stop rabbiting on in a moment or two and he would get some peace. *Yes! Yes!* he nodded. *I understand completely. Don't worry,* he seemed to say...but in truth whatever she was now saying was totally lost on him. Not that it mattered – she would undoubtedly repeat it all three or four times before she went out the door. When she paused to draw breath, George got up from the breakfast table and shambled off to the study. He started tidying papers into different stacks, lifting up books and putting them down, switching the computer on to standby, trying to give the impression that he was keen to follow his wife's orders. The more convincing he looked, the quicker she would go out and leave him in peace. He opened a desk draw to surreptitiously check if his whisky flask was there, hiding beneath a number of business cards and a forest of pens and pencils. Yep – and it was still half full. Bliss! He shovelled a couple of papers into the draw and then shut it, glancing round as if to say: *Look! I've started the clean-up...*

Annabel's monologue was still continuing but drawing to a close. Cats and rose beds were being reprised. The delivery of provisions from Tesco's was now past its fourth chapter. George followed his wife into the hallway, his face bright and compliant, his eyes looking expectantly at the front door. Only a few minutes more of this to survive. He could almost feel his study chair beneath him and taste the whisky as he shuffled forward to open the door for his departing spouse.

"And lastly, George, don't try and fool me into thinking you're working on that computer of yours. Last time you fell asleep there at your desk and I swear there was alcohol on your breath. I don't know where you get it from, you drunken reprobate, but if you fall asleep and miss the deliveries this morning I'm sure I'll turn you out of the house and throw your laptop after you..."

George tried to smile obligingly but only managed a strangled grimace; he held back the front door and escorted his partner in life out of the house, doing his best to ensure she had left nothing behind. He nodded and waved goodbye and then at last he could shut his wife and the rest of the world out and retire immediately, making hot-foot for the study like a greyhound out of the traps.

Yes, a greyhound, he liked that image. He reached his chair and leant back in it, whisky flask in hand, and thought about that dog and her precocious, immoderate owner. As the liquid burned its way south, he dreamt about that woman for the umpteenth time. She was altogether too dangerous to be let loose. No doubt about it. Her dog was perfectly acceptable: friendly without being too forward; beautiful to look at; athletic, and with not an ounce of fat on her frame to slow her down. George noticed the bitch floated effortlessly over the ground when she cantered away. But her owner was the one who should have been on a lead – very forthright, unrestrained in her opinions and possessed of an altogether far too provocative geometry. Extremely dangerous! She could start a fight in monastery, that one.

George took another swig from his flask and relaxation spread all through his body from his stomach outward. He put his feet up on the desk and idly gazed outside the study window into the garden. If he had his way that garden would be altogether wilder, greener, less manicured, and with no bloody standard roses. There was something offensive about having roses trained to grow up and suddenly burst into flower, waist height, at the top of a vertical stem. Too domesticated. Artificial. Like lollipops, and their colours just as artificial.

Another gulp of whisky. George lingered there for five minutes savouring the moment before deciding to swing his legs down and get up, a little wobbly, to take a tour of the garden. He went through the kitchen to the back door with half a mind to take the bread knife with him and commit murder: to saw through every damn standard rose stem on his tour. But then, standing on the back doorstep, looking out, he thought better of it. Annabel would never forgive him. Several headless stems could never be explained away as some sort of accident or natural disaster and he had no justifiable excuse for such a slaughterous plan of action other than he didn't like expurgated nature: trained, controlled, defanged and thoroughly tamed.

He stepped out into the middle of the weedless lawn; a sculpted patch of green that – under instructions – he had mowed in straight, well-behaved lines. He suddenly had an insane urge to cut loose and go on the rampage, trampling the flower beds, chopping down the roses and flinging the debris to all quarters. He realised with a dreadful, sinking feeling that it wasn't so much the garden that had been tamed; it was him.

A voice broke through into his consciousness. "Hello, George! Lovely blooms, aren't they? Is Annabel there?"

It was Stephen Maxwell, the next-door neighbour but one. Smarmy Stephen – the world's best horticulturist and sycophant who was always enticing Annabel into his immaculate, distastefully ordered property and enthusing about ever more extravagant decorations and alterations for the garden. His latest acquisition was a three-tier fountain with little fat cherubs at the top spouting water. *Grotesque!* George was sure that his wife would want one of those soon.

"No, no, she's at the hairdressers," George replied through gritted teeth.

"Well, old top, do tell her to call round when she's back. Patio plants need looking after as the weather warms up, don't you know!" Stephen gave an ingratiating, totally false smile that made George's stomach turn but, polite as ever, he just nodded his agreement and lowered his eyes. There was somebody who could do with being looked after, he thought. George had visions of beating him around the head with a garden spade, but he merely moved to inspect the nearest flower bed beside him, trying to give the impression of someone who knew something about gardening and needed no advice from an over-enthusiastic neighbour.

As he did so, there was a tiny explosion of spitting and screeching and a tabby cat vaulted out of Smarmy Stephen's garden with the latter trying to hit it with an old brush. Stephen's language was certainly not controlled and immaculate. He held the brush up and shook it vindictively in the air.

"Damned filthy feline! Trying to shit all over the place and ruin all my hard work. I'll wring its bloody neck if I don't batter it to death first!"

The cat stopped halfway across the intervening garden between the two men and looked back and snarled at its assailant. It then continued crossing over towards George, leaping over the wooden fence that separated them to drop on all fours below him and then wind itself around the legs of this rather more welcoming human.

The cat was now out of sight of Smarmy Stephen but not out of his mind. "Where's it gone now? If you can see that moggy over there, then do me a favour and spear it with a garden fork or something, will you? Anything to keep it away from our gardens. It's a bloody menace!"

"It's Mr Tibbs who belongs to that little old lady over the back," replied George defensively. "I don't think she'd be too pleased if any harm came to it."

"Then she should either chain it up in her own garden or not let it out in the first place. I tell you, if it comes in here again I'll kill it. And Annabel's of the same opinion, I know. Your wife would be pleased to see the end of it, same as I would."

George looked down at Tibbs the cat, now purring and rubbing itself against his ankles. "Yes, yes," he replied, discouraging any further comment. He knelt down by the side of the wooden fence, out of Smarmy Stephen's eye-line and fondled the tabby cat, stroking its head and rubbing behind its ears. He whispered soothing words to it as if to tell it not to be so frightened and to take care and stay out of trouble. Then he started whistling absent-mindedly and busied about amongst the flower beds, again simulating what he hoped looked like a devoted gardener. Smarmy Stephen went back into his own house and left him to it.

Chapter 2

All next weekend was the occasion of the County Agricultural Show. Annabel had agreed with Smarmy Stephen to meet up on Sunday afternoon and spend several hours in the horticultural section. Fine, George would wander off to inspect various animals, farm machines, outdoor wear and, especially, the refreshment tent – or tents. There was sure to be numerous real ales from around the region and further afield, not to mention countless varieties of single malt whisky.

As soon as he parked his old jalopy as directed in the designated field, he saw Smarmy Stephen heading for them. George groaned. His neighbour was wearing his trousers rather slackly around the waist, or rather around his buttocks, supposedly because he wanted to look cool and ape the fashions of a younger generation, except that wearing his trousers as if they were falling down was not now fashionable and just made him look like an idiot. George hoped he tripped over in them into a pile of manure.

"Hallo, Annabel, I saw your motor coming in – glad you could make it!" Stephen's voice entered by the side window.

"Oh, Stevie, I do wish George would get something more elegant to drive around in. It's so embarrassing being seen in this ancient pile." Annabel didn't like old Land Rovers.

"Sorry, dear. The Bentley showrooms were shut the last time I was down in London," George remarked sardonically.

"That's quite enough of that!" Annabel reacted sharply. "Since you cannot conduct a reasonable conversation I shall go home with Stevie this afternoon. He has a new Renault that I am not ashamed to be driven in."

"Please yourself." George pecked his wife on the cheek. "You two go off and roll around amongst the shrubbery. I'll take a look at the prize cattle. More my sort of society."

Annabel snorted and descended from the Land Rover into the arms of her neighbour. She wasn't sure whether George was being sarcastic or not. She could never read his odd comments. Was he being deliberately annoying, or simply perverse, or was he bumbling about on another planet as usual? Did he mind her announced preference for another man's company? Had he even noticed?

George was indifferent to his wife's confusion. He just left her to it, locked up the Land Rover, pocketed the keys and wandered off; whistling to himself, looking about amiably at what the County Show had to offer.

Ancient breeds of cattle and sheep he passed by. A tent selling various items of footwear: wellington boots in all shapes and sizes, walkers' shoes and even traditional slippers. He paused and browsed at each stall and enclosure, happily bumbling about with no specific goal in mind and most of the day now at his disposal. He negotiated a stretch of muddy pathway and a family of four dancing round it, plus a couple of enthusiastic black Labradors, before he came next upon the main showground with a programme pinned up alongside it. Apparently in an hour or so there was going to be a parade of horse-drawn carriages circling the field. But that wasn't what George was looking for. Then across the other side of the roped-off showground he spied the first refreshment tent. There were a number of people milling around outside and the sound they made that came across to him seemed decidedly jolly. That was definitely the place to be! He set off on a roundabout route to get there.

Three-quarters of the way to his destination, where the sound of laughter, animated conversation and the occasional dog barking assailed his ears, where he could just begin to smell the alcohol being exhaled in the late spring air, a sandy-coloured greyhound came leaping towards him in a whirl of long legs, whiplash tail and bright eyes.

"Hello! It's Rosie, isn't it?" George put his hands down to caress his affectionate friend. He dared not glance round to find her owner.

"Well, look who it is here – Rosie's found her circus friend again!"

George straightened up and struck an indignant air of one who has been falsely slandered.

"Ahem! I have told you, young woman, I have nothing to do with circuses!" Rosie gave a slight whimper and pushed her nose into George's hand as if to console him.

"Oh pouf!" Carol retorted. "Don't tell me you are an accountant because I won't believe you. Sally..." she turned to a nubile companion, "look at this man. He's trying to hide behind some staid and conservative image but it is as plain as Rosie's wet nose that he is a dog's best friend and clearly a habitué of a circus, or the jungle, or somewhere similar..."

"Maybe a zoo?" Sally ventured. "He does have a sort of subdued, suppressed animal spirit about him."

"Mmm. Hadn't thought of that. Are you a zookeeper?"

"Certainly not! I am an accountant with a solid reputation and I never frequent circuses, jungles or zoos, and nor do I assail strangers in the street, accusing them of wild or outrageous employments. You should be ashamed of yourselves!"

"My! He has something of a temper, doesn't he?" remarked Sally to her friend.

"Yes," replied Carol, rising to the tirade directed against her, "and as for accusations, I have never assailed any stranger on any street...but if you remember it was Rosie who introduced me to you on a footpath not so very far from here. And I was proper enough to introduce myself and tell you my name, to which you have not yet responded and I think that is very impolite of you. I've a good mind to report you to the police as someone who hassles young women..."

George's face rose in colour and he looked alarmedly about

him. "Me? Hassling? But, but it was you…"

"What do you think, Sally? Something of a wild man? A danger to girls out alone? Do you think the police would swallow that?"

"Oh easily! He still hasn't told you his name, d'ya notice? Obviously has something to hide. A criminal record even…"

"This is absolutely unforgiveable. I was just going over there for a drink and you two set upon me and try to ruin my reputation. Madam…"

"Carol!" Carol interjected

"Carol…you have a very friendly dog and I'm pleased to make her acquaintance, but it was never my intention – before or now – to press my attentions any further…"

"Oooh," said Sally, "watch out, Carol, he's pressing his attentions!"

"Aaaagh!" George went purple.

"Do you think he is dangerous, Sally? Really? Or do you think we should go and have a drink and keep an eye on him? Keep him from molesting any innocent young girls around here. We might even get his name and details; get the police to run a check on him, perhaps…"

George realised he was getting nowhere with these two young women and anything he said would no doubt be taken down and used as evidence against him. He gently pushed Rosie the greyhound to one side and struck out in the direction of the refreshment tent, followed by two smiling attendants and a dog. On reaching the bar, he ordered a double malt whisky, choosing The MaCallan from a row of bottles, only to hear his new companions requesting vodka cocktails to add to his order. He turned to scowl at them but was met by winning smiles and the suggestion that they sit together at a table where Rosie had space to lie beside them. George gave up. He wasn't going to argue anymore.

"C'mon then! Open up! Who are you and why do you have

such an effect on my dog?" Carol was smiling broadly and offering George space to breathe, instead of sailing into battle straight away.

"My name is George Potts, I'm an accountant and I've never met such disgraceful, abandoned young women in all my life!"

"Oh that's nothing. We've been remarkably restrained so far, haven't we, Sally." Carol grinned. "I mean, you've still got your trousers on, haven't you?"

"Good grief! What next? Wherever do you get this attitude from – accosting poor, unsuspecting blokes like me all alone in broad daylight. You should be locked up!"

"Well, actually," whispered Sally, leaning across, "you're lucky. We normally go out the two of us together with bull mastiffs and rottweilers, looking to set upon any single fellers, dirty old men, flashers and the like that we find. Us women gotta get our own back, gettit?"

"Well, really!" George downed his whisky, barely tasting it. He was shocked for a moment…until he saw the laughing eyes of his two companions. He stood up.

"I've drunk that whisky far too quickly, thanks to you two. I'm going to get another now while I've still got my clothes on. How are you two fixed?"

"Well that's more neighbourly of you," said Carol. "I'm alright thanks. You, Sally?"

"No thanks," smiled Sally. "But do come back. We won't assault you, honest!"

George nodded and went off and ordered another double MaCallan. He returned to the table and carefully arranged his long limbs so that they would not interfere with any feminine ones and give the wrong impression. There were certainly some luscious female limbs on display about him. Not tracksuited this time, but some very tight denims that left little to the imagination. George struggled to keep his imagination in check. He took a sip of whisky and rolled it around inside his mouth, determined to get the full flavour of it this time. He was still a little red in the face and he desperately tried not to let his eyes wander over the figures of these two spirited sirens. At last he began to relax. George dropped a hand to fondle Rosie's head and neck.

"So tell us, George – how do you do it? Rosie had never met you before but within seconds she was treating you like a long-lost friend. And look at her now. Instant love!"

"Yeah," Sally butted in. "I don't think attacking him with rottweilers would be of much use. Their great big jaws would probably end up kissing him!"

"I've always liked dogs...in fact, all animals. It's probably because I've never been allowed to have one that I seem to ooze affection in their direction. I knew a woman once who couldn't have babies. She gurgled and googled at just about any infant that crossed her path. Same for me and dogs."

"What do you mean – you've never been allowed to have a dog?!" Carol asked. "You're a grown man, aren't you? A staid and conservative pillar of society. What's stopping you if you want one?"

"The wife hates 'em."

"Oh dear!"

"So that's what accounts for the subdued, repressed expression then!"

"Not at all. I am *not* repressed – just considerate of my wife's feelings..."

"Oh, George, you *need* a dog – or a tiger, or some suitable beast that reflects your true character. Don't you think so, Sally? It's obvious. We can both see it in you."

"Absolutely. This is tragic. George, you have to be unchained!"

"I know what – I'll go round and speak to his wife. That's what I'll do. George – tell me your home address!"

"I'll do nothing of the sort...and neither will you. I can't have either of you anywhere near my wife, or near where I live. Two wild and riotous females like you. What would the neighbours think?"

"They've probably not had an original thought in their heads for years, going by your reaction. George, I am mightily disappointed in you. In fact, you ought to be mightily disappointed in yourself, too. You've simply got to cut loose and do something worth living for…before you stop living altogether."

George downed his whisky yet again, forgetting to taste it properly, yet again. These two had got right under his skin. How could they size him up so quickly when he barely knew them? It seemed that in a few moments they knew more about him than he knew himself. Looking at them, these two lively and gorgeous women, he realised that they represented all that he had missed out in life, and they instinctively knew that. Lovely-looking creatures, so confident and sure of themselves and no doubt they had no reservations in going out and getting whatever they wanted in life, whereas George had reined himself in and bottled-up his desires for decades. Was it really so obvious? And what *did* he really want in life? He hadn't asked himself that question for so long that he had forgotten what he had once dreamed about when he was a young man. *Now look at me,* he thought. *Old before my time. Stuck in a rut.* Peace and quiet was all he wanted these days. Nothing more. Well, these two were certainly shaking that up!

George's face was a struggle of emotions. Carol suddenly softened at the sight of him, leant across and lightly took hold of his hand. George's emotions went into even more turmoil. What were they doing to him? He took his hand away, looked down and fondled Rosie the greyhound once more. He couldn't speak and nor could he look up just yet, his eyes were welling up.

Carol spoke up brightly to fill the sudden hiatus that had occurred: "Sally, we have our next project sitting here in front of us. We have to do our good deed for society. By the look of it, it's gonna take quite some time, but there is hidden potential in this man and it's our duty to release it. The world will undoubtedly benefit from his talent when it is fully released, don't you think?"

"Spot on, Carol! Hidden depths here that should remain hidden no longer. How are we going to get at them?"

"George, listen to me. We've got to see you again, do you hear? Soon. Here's where I work..." Carol scribbled an address down on a piece of paper and passed it across the table. "I finish around five pm each day, so you can find me leaving here at that time every day next week. I'll be looking out for you each day, gottit? And if I don't see you by Friday next then I'll come searching for you. And I'll find you, believe me. In fact Sally and I will dance naked in the road outside your house, calling out your name all the time, won't we, Sal? So you'd better see me before next weekend, OK? Or all the neighbours will have something to talk about for the rest of the year..."

Sally looked at her companion. "He said he has a solid reputation, Carol. I wonder how long that will last."

"Ladies! Please! Behave yourselves..."

"We will, George, so long as you do, too. See you sometime next week, alright?" Carol raised her glass and winked at Sally to do the same. There was just a smear of whisky remaining in George's glass but he grimaced and raised it also – a symbolic gesture. For good or ill, he was now committed to spend some time with these irrepressible young women and he had no idea where that would lead.

Chapter 3

George spent the next hour wandering around the Agricultural Show in a daze. He'd said goodbye to his two tormentors but, of course, they were not finished with him yet – they kept bumping into him in the enclosure for horses; by the prize-bull pen; at the sheepdog display and then finally in another refreshment tent where George was driven to sample more whisky.

As George ambled out of the tent, Carol stopped him in his tracks.

"George, how are you getting home? You can't drive with all that whisky inside of you!"

"'Course I can!" he blustered. "Nothin' to it. I'm perfectly OK and it's only a couple of miles to go, anyway…"

"Don't be ridiculous, George. You've had at least three doubles that I've seen. That's six whiskies and I don't know how many other drinks you may have had. Your reactions will be all over the place; you'd be a menace to all other traffic as well as to yourself."

"Not near enough a menace to all and sundry as you and your friend!"

"Now you're being facetious. Don't try and change the subject. You can't drive, George. You mustn't even think of it. You'll end up in a ditch, or in hospital."

"No I won't. What is it with you and your friend? What have I done to deserve you? You've been hounding me all afternoon and you've threatened to do it probably most of next week as well…do you enjoy torturing innocent strangers?" Carol and Sally had unlocked some deep down emotion within him, and with an hour's mulling over it plus the whisky loosening his inhibitions, George was feeling very fragile.

"You're not a stranger and I'm not torturing you – just trying to save yourself from getting killed, or injured, or taken into hospital, or thrown into prison. George, honestly, you cannot get behind a wheel in your state. Give me the keys and I'll drive you home! Sally will follow behind in her car."

"And have you find out where I live? You'll never leave me in peace if I do that."

"We'd find out and not leave you in peace, anyway," butted in Sally with a grin. "So you might just as well hand over the keys. C'mon, George, let us look after you!"

"Please, George." Carol held on to his arm and searched his face. Sally was looking at him; Rosie too.

"Oh, bloody hell!" He delved into his pocket for the keys. Of course they were right. He had entirely forgotten about driving, what with everything else on his mind, and had these two not accosted him he would have been in a proper fix about getting home, so they were actually proposing an easy solution. He had to put up a show of resistance, though, however sensible their demands. He couldn't just let them trample all over him without some protest or other. In the short time he had known these girls, he was determined to try and exert some modicum of control over the situation. He couldn't allow them to have it all their own way all the time.

He led the two, wandering a little, across to the car park field and towards the Land Rover. As he was doing so he noticed that Smarmy Stephen's new Renault was still there. Well, at least that meant he could collapse in his own home without battling any more females. He staggered on to reach his own motor.

"Is this your chariot, George?" cried Carol. "Well, that's more like it! Rugged, battered, full of character...just what you *should* have! You're not at all a hopeless case, after all!"

George couldn't resist a tiny smile. A very different reaction to that of Annabel. "Do you like it then?"

"Oh absolutely, George," chorused Sally. "This is precisely the sort of wheels that we could have ordered for you. A bit old, cantankerous, no concession whatever to things fashionable but definitely a bit on the wild side and ready to go off into the wide blue yonder at the slightest invitation. Isn't that so, Carol?"

"Certainly! This is decidedly *not* an accountant's car. Nothing like it. George: we love you for this...and I can't wait to drive it. Gimme the keys!"

Rosie was let into the back; Carol got into the driver's seat and George clambered slowly into the passenger seat. The car park field seemed to be swirling all around him as he did so. He had a little trouble focusing on what he was doing.

Carol switched on and the Land Rover roared into life. She grinned out of the window at Sally and then across at George.

"Oh look, Sal: *three* gear levers in pretty colours – red, yellow and black. I wonder which one I should use first..."

"The black one," growled George. "Don't touch the others or you'll never get me home."

Carol laughed. "Alright, I've got it sorted." She engaged first gear and lurched forward, calling out to Sally as she did so, "I'll go slowly at first 'til I get the hang of this. Catch me up, Sal!"

George relaxed and closed his eyes as the Land Rover crept forward, Carol spinning the wheel and directing them towards the exit. He wasn't sure whether he liked this or not – having this independent, unpredictable and extremely sensuous young female take him for a ride. As he pondered this, he felt a long wet nose interfere with his right ear and looking back, his gaze disappeared into the dark, round eyes of Rosie the greyhound: Rosie, the one who had started all this; Rosie, who was now demonstrating some canine concern for her semi-comatose human friend. George decided that there was something definitely magical about this hound. She had introduced him to her owner, an unstoppable force of nature, under whose spell he seemed to have fallen almost willingly. It was Rosie who had sought him out and stopped him in his wanderings and summoned him to take another direction and he was crazy enough to go along with it: last weekend and this one too, and who knows where next week.

Chapter 3

The Land Rover bumped its way over the rutted field and out onto the main road. "OK, George, which way now?" Carol asked.

"Head south," said George, waking up. "And when you get to the roundabout, take the first turn-off that leads you left, towards the village."

Two cars, a battered old Land Rover and a sporty red mini, motored along together until a little time later they eventually reached a row of garages at the back of a terrace of Victorian houses at the north end of the village. George directed his chauffeur to stop and leave their chariot where it was. Sally drew up behind and so all got out and assembled between the two vehicles on the tarmac in front of the garages.

George gave his thanks to the two drivers and their dog. "Excuse me if I do not invite you in to my humble dwelling place but firstly I think I need to lie down and sleep after this somewhat exhausting encounter; secondly, I wouldn't want the neighbours to get the slightest hint of the disreputable company I am at present consorting with; and thirdly, I fear the consequences of what you would get up to if I let you in. I hope you don't mind?"

"We quite understand, George. No offence taken. And we have plenty of time in the future to ruin your reputation and ransack your property, haven't we, Sally?"

"Indubitably!"

"And thank you, George, for being such an adorable sport!"

"Yes – just think of the fun and games we can all have together in the weeks to come!" added Sally.

George groaned. He started forward as if to say goodbye but Carol held up a hand.

"You do have that address with you still, don't you, George? You wouldn't want to forget to come and meet me after work, would you?"

George fumbled in his trouser pocket. He hadn't read it yet but he found it curled up, half forgotten, buried in amongst a paper handkerchief. He waved it in front of his newfound associate.

"Yes, yes! Here it is. Now off you go and leave me in peace!"

Carol and Sally both embraced him, emphasising that he had better get as much peace as he could now, since it would not last. George nodded resignedly and bent down to give one last caress to Rosie, the magical greyhound. Then he watched them all get into the mini and drive off.

He sighed. He walked over to open his garage, got into the Land Rover and parked it in its rightful home. He shut it all up and then turned to go into his back garden via the back gate. He looked at the address he had been given and, halfway up the back garden path, he stopped.

"Bloody hell!" he exclaimed.

The address he had been given was that of St Bartholomew's College, in Durham. Carol worked in the same college as that of his wife.

George made straight for the desk draw in the study. Six whiskies or not, he was still too sober to take in this latest shock to his system. He upended the flask.

"Bloody hell!" he exclaimed again, louder, as if the first time wasn't enough to signal the horror that he felt enveloping him. "They must know each other!"

The college had been expanding and taking on more staff and students and George was willing to bet that Carol must be one of a new intake – with that personality he would have been certain to have heard of her from his wife who had been working there for decades. Come to think of it, he remembered at the beginning of the academic year that Annabel had been cursing the influence of a number of new faces in the college who had come in like tornadoes, seemingly hired by the Master to shake things up. Carol was certainly a force of nature equal to any tornado.

My God! He had promised to go down and meet this new and far-too-sensual young woman on the road outside the college at about the same time that his own, somewhat more serious and censorious mate would be emerging. This was impossible! He couldn't do that now. Yet what would happen if, instead, the doorbell rang and this unrestrained and undomesticated wild woman confronted them both in their own house? Equally impossible!

George tipped up the whisky flask once more. No way out! It seemed as if he was caught, whichever way he turned. Foggy-headed by now, this was a dilemma that George could not resolve for the moment. He blundered his way into the kitchen and tried to make himself a ham and cheese sandwich – an endeavour which required a certain degree of manual dexterity that for the time being had deserted him. Surveying the mess he had created, he picked up the debris as best he could, put it on a plate and tried not to lose his way into the lounge, despite the wall doing its best to bump into him and spill his platter as he ventured forth. George found his favourite armchair in front of the television and arranged himself in it, although he discovered his various limbs would not go quite where he wanted them to. It seemed as if they belonged to someone else. He tried to eat the sandwich-cum-disaster that he had made. He got some down before the fog in his head swirled thicker and thicker and overcast clouds drew a curtain across his mind.

It was dark when his wife tripped over his sprawling figure on her way in from the back garden. Annabel cursed out loud and George, out of habit, went immediately into defensive mode. He apologised to the unseen figure in the blackness and withdrew his legs. Brushing a collection of breadcrumbs and other assorted foodstuffs off his chest he struggled to his feet and, back under automatic pilot, he tottered out into the kitchen. Ignoring, not even hearing the various indecorous comments made in his direction by his beloved spouse, he did his best to clear things away and then turned somnolently to climb the stairs and go to bed. There, he descended into a silent black hole, illuminated briefly by a bitch with magical eyes into which he gazed hypnotically until the spark deep therein them suddenly snuffed out. He slept.

Birds were singing the morning chorus at full pelt when George next awoke. There was obviously a competition going on between rival blackbirds somewhere as to who would get through to the man of this house soonest. George lay immobile, scarcely able to believe it. The sun had not yet fully risen, his head felt unusually strange, not an insect in the house had stirred but a football crowd of birds outside were determined to rehearse every song in their vast repertoire in their efforts to wake him up. George grunted. He uttered sounds that had never before issued from his throat. He was not a happy man.

But he could not go back to sleep now; his brain wouldn't let him. Eyes barely focusing, his head complaining, George tried to disentangle himself from beneath the bedcovers and, in doing so, he only succeeded in finding himself on all fours on the carpet beside the bed. He looked round. He gasped. In the full-length mirror he caught sight of a greyhound in the bedroom! He uttered not a sound. It wouldn't do to wake the wife, sleeping soundly in her own bed on the other side of the room. But what an animal looked back at him! Not a sandy-coloured bitch like Rosie but a taller, big-chested black-coated male with a long white bib running down his front. A handsome beast...though as he looked at him, George thought the dog's eyes did look a little dazed.

"Like my own," he considered. "I wonder if it's been at the whisky?"

Did dogs drink spirits? George wondered as he looked down and prepared to get up from the floor where he had tumbled out of bed.

He stopped moving. Staring down, instead of his arms holding him up, he saw two slim, black dog's legs immediately below him. Dog's legs with paws, not hands. Putting his head down, George looked back under his body and there, at the back of him were two more dog's legs. With paws, not feet.

George sat down with a plop and examined the mirror. There was the black greyhound sitting on its haunches, staring back. George put his head on one side, puzzled by this vision in front of him. The dog with dazed eyes put his head on one side also. George raised a front paw and scratched his head. So did the greyhound in the mirror. George said hello out loud to himself. Well, to his ears he reckoned it was hello but it actually sounded like: "Wuff!"

"Hmmm," said George to himself. "This is rich. Seems like I've changed into a greyhound overnight." To say that this was a novel turn of events was something of an understatement. George had been drunk before. He had passed out before; but whenever he had come-to in the past he had always come-to as the same sort of person, all be it a little more dishevelled, as he had been earlier. He had never changed species before, at least he thought he hadn't; his memory clearly was not at its best yet.

George turned and examined himself more closely, trying to get his eyes to behave as they should. Yep, a tall, black dog…and very well-equipped by the sight of it, he reckoned, lifting a leg to display his masculine parts. He was pleased with what he saw. He slowly commenced some doggy exercises: bending down; sitting up; twisting this way and that; learning to control his various limbs, joints and muscles, seeing if any creaked and groaned like he was accustomed to in his human form. Great! Everything seemed to be in perfect working order. But enough of the self-examination; this was early morning and George needed to have a pee.

Problem: how to do that?

George padded out to the bathroom. The door was closed to, but thankfully not shut. George inserted a nose in the small gap between door and door jamb and pushed. He entered the bathroom. The toilet seat was up. But how was he going to do this? He tried to get up and sit on the toilet but he slid suddenly backwards and for one awful moment he thought he would end up getting stuck in the pan – half in, half out. George gave a cry of horror – but it was a strangled canine howl which he instantly stopped in mid-flow. There was no way he wanted to wake Annabel. With a scrabbling of feet, George got back off the toilet and tried to figure a better way to answer nature's call. He was a tall dog, fortunately. Nothing for it – he sidled up, lifted a leg and aimed as best as he could, doggy style, over the top of the porcelain and into the interior of mankind's most sanitary convenience. Aaah, relief! When he'd done, he examined the result. George was a careful, fastidious creature – both as man and dog. He wasn't one to wave his wand to all parts, shaking the drops off everywhere and leaving his mark for others to clean up. How'd he do this time? Not bad, if he said so himself. Unaccustomed as he was to relieving himself as dogs do, he had managed to aim pretty well and hit the target with no extraneous incriminating evidence. George was proud of himself. So early in his dog's life and already he had established unerring control of his masterful physique. He lifted a paw and pressed the flush. Job done!

Next on his mind was breakfast. George sallied forth from the en-suite bathroom, out of the bedroom (the bedroom door was never shut – Annabel didn't like being closed in with her husband) and then he scampered down the stairs and into the kitchen below. Eggs and bacon was definitely not going to happen, but what else could he eat? He wasn't sure what his taste buds would approve of in his new quadruped form – eggs and bacon did seem attractive but he reluctantly had to try and forget about that. What else? Most of the food seemed to be stored in cabinets way above his head. Beneath the sink were only detergents, cleaning materials, various polishes and bin-liners. No joy there. George reached his front paws up onto the kitchen counter and cleaned up various bits of bread, ham and cheese that he had left there the night before. Hmmm, they tasted alright. He wasn't so keen on the cheese, though. He got back down and searched in the lounge. More debris from his pseudo-sandwich was scattered on the floor about the armchair. He hoovered those up. Annabel would be pleased, he thought. But he was still hungry.

The fridge! He had to get inside and see what treasures he could gain access to there. It took a little while before his front paws could get purchase on the fridge door. These appliances were certainly not dog-friendly, he surmised – probably by design. But after scrabbling about for an age he managed to get his nose inside and now – what was there he could open?

Fortunately, the plastic wrapper in which the ham had been packaged had been savaged by drunken hands only a few hours ago and so for a determined greyhound with an inquiring tongue it was not difficult to finish off the contents. He smacked his lips. That felt better! Now – there was a carton of milk that was open and half full. Did he fancy that? Well he wasn't a cat – perish the thought – but he'd give it a try. In this case it was impossible to drink the contents without spilling any – just trying to pick it up in his jaws meant squeezing a fair shower all over the place but he nonetheless drank most of it and, again, housetrained as he was, he could lick up much of the milk that was scattered around in various puddles.

George sat down and took stock of progress so far. Had he eaten and drank his fill? Yes, he thought so. He'd managed to invade this manmade reserve and satisfy his most basic needs and if he wanted any more he reckoned he could always come back. Today was Monday and the house would be empty as Annabel and he would be out at work.

Work? He couldn't go to work as he was. No matter that he prided himself on being an athletic, handsome and intelligent greyhound, adept at finding his way around the house, he could hardly sit in his office at work and function normally as an accountant. Mind, that was an interesting thought. Could he do that? He could still read OK – the ingredients and instructions on the milk carton made sense as they always did – he could presumably still analyse a balance sheet and make decisions on the basis of what he saw...but communicating with others would be a problem, presuming that they would let a black greyhound into his office in the first place. No, they never would. He should stop thinking about that.

Could he handle a computer? That might be possible. Interesting word: 'handle' – this was clearly related to the word 'hand' and as such discriminated against all creatures without such appendages. Minority groups should protest about such discriminatory language! Why couldn't he *pawdle* a computer? He'd give it a go.

George trotted into his study and got onto his chair. He reached a paw across to switch on his laptop. So far so good. But the mouse was not at all helpful. Disconnect that. His long and pointed jaw could achieve that, at the risk of ripping out the wire and its connection. No problem, all done safely without any damage. Now the keyboard...hmmm. It took a lot of trial and error and much discipline on his part but George could eventually switch on, find his way through to his e-mails and send a message to his employers. He thought carefully how he could send an essential message in as few words as possible. This was it: *Very sick. Will come in when I can. Potts.*

Getting that written took almost an hour. The capitals were the most difficult to pawdle but he was determined to do it and make it look as genuine as possible. Then he switched off and retreated from the study. It was time to go out and greet the day. A bright spring morning was calling unrestrainedly to this new dog on the block. What adventures awaited him outside?

Chapter 4

George appraised the back door. Getting out was no problem, just depress the handle, but once he was in the garden it would not be easy to return – the door could only be opened from the outside by a key. Well – nothing for it but to take his keys outside and bury them somewhere in the hope that, if the door was shut and he wanted to return, he could somehow solve that problem if and when it arose. George lifted the keys from his desk in his mouth, ran up to the back door, pawed the handle down, and sauntered out into the morning.

The back garden was far too ordered and arty-farty for any self-respecting canine. He looked about to see where a dog might bury a bone, or bunch of keys. Near the back gate, where the dustbin resided behind a little fence of its own (ugh!), there was a patch of bare earth where Annabel would never tread, nor think to plant a flower. George got his front paws into it and scratched away until he had dug a reasonable hiding place. He dropped the keys in and then turned to cover it up. As he finished doing this he noticed a movement in the garden next door, or rather, along the top of the fence that separated that garden from Smarmy Stephen's.

A rush of adrenalin surged through George's veins. He was now a greyhound, a sight hound – a breeding stock trained over millennia to chase any smaller creature on sight. In a split second he found himself flying down the garden path, leaping over the first fence and straight-way bounding over the next with the cat dead-centre in his radar. He caught it hiding behind Smarmy Stephen's grotesque fountain. The cat was cornered and rose up on all fours, hairs standing on end, spitting and swearing and doing everything in its power to save its life.

George skidded to a halt. What was he doing? He had no intention on ripping this poor animal apart, despite every doggy instinct within him egging him on.

The cat interpreted this pause as a sign of weakness on his assailant's behalf. "Yes, back off, you fiend – before I scratch your eyes out!"

George smirked. This was of course sheer bravado on the cat's part, but he had to respect this feisty feline – staring death in the face but determined to go down fighting.

"Sorry, puss!" George apologised. "Dunno what came over me for a moment but I don't mean you any harm. Really…I guess I just wanted to play."

"Don't you 'puss' me, you monster," came back the cat, spiritedly. "And don't pretend you want to play games – I can guess the sort of bloodthirsty games you like. You're not taking me without a fight!"

"No, no, you don't get it. I *know* you. I like you. Any enemy of Smarmy Stephen is a friend of mine."

The cat looked at him suspiciously. "Waddya mean? You know me? I've never seen you before in my life…and what's this about Smarmy Stephen?"

George sat down on his back quarters – hardly a threatening pose – and tried to reassure his furry friend. "Yes, I know you – you're Mr Tibbs and you belong to the lady over the back. And Smarmy Stephen here hates having you amongst his roses and will gladly strangle you if given a chance. You ran off into my garden last week to escape him. Don't you remember I stroked and looked after you?"

"That was George. He's alright, he is. Can't stand his lady, mind."

"That was me. I'm George. I'm a greyhound now."

Mr Tibbs was quite taken by this news. "Oh yeah? Since when?"

"Since I woke up this morning. I was George the man yesterday. I'm Greyhound George today."

"An' what you gonna be tomorrow? A friggin' cart horse?"

"I dunno about tomorrow, and there's no call for that language. I don't mean you any harm so there's no need to get all catty with me!"

"Can't much do anything else, me. I don't claim to change from one animal to another like you...but you're right, I've got no cause to act insulting. It's just that you gave me the fright of my life."

"Sorry, like I said. I'm still learning about my doggy side. I've never had the urge to chase cats before!"

"Well, my reactions are usually pretty quick but this Smarmy Stephen, as you call him, he damn near broke my leg yesterday, hurling a stone at me. So you caught me before I could get away...an' you're telling me you were George yesterday?"

"I'm still George today...only different."

"I can see that."

"Smarmy Stephen hurt you?"

"Yeah, caught me on the back leg here when I wasn't looking. The bastard! It only makes me even more determined to shit in his garden!"

"Good for you, Tibbs!" George was struck by an idea. He was goodness knows how many times bigger than his feline partner in crime and if he summoned it up he was sure he could leave Smarmy Stephen a much bigger reminder of his presence than any cat. He looked about for the prime location for his intended present. He asked for Mr Tibbs' opinion since the cat was a more frequent visitor to this location than he.

"An interesting question, George." Mr Tibbs had now been won over by his larger companion. "As an artistic feature, slap bang in the middle of the circular lawn there would the ideal spot that many would recommend...but I'm of the opinion that it is not art but sheer, bloody-minded revenge that is of the order of the day. In which case, why not *there* – just outside the back door where he's likely to step out unawares right into the middle of it? Yes. That's definitely the place: X marks the spot!"

Smarmy Stephen had a new doormat outside his backdoor with his own name: *S. Maxwell* emblazoned upon it. How pretentious! It was just asking for it. George padded over to the back door and poised himself carefully over the mat. He shook his behind as if to encourage his rear end to do its business. He was conscious that his toiletry aim so far today had been spot on and he wanted to maintain a one hundred per cent record.

Mr Tibbs was much impressed. "Go, George!" he called out. "Stand and deliver!"

George had not eaten much recently so it was a bit of a sweat but determination won the day and it wasn't long before the X spot was covered.

"Bull's-eye!" called out Mr Tibbs. "Well done, George! Turn round and admire your work."

George did as he was bid. *S. Maxwell* was now more like *S. MooOwell.* For the second time that morning, George was proud of his physical prowess. If this was a dog's life, he was beginning to enjoy it.

"OK, Tibbs, time to get out of here and leave Smarmy Stephen to it. That'll teach him not to attack us poor dumb creatures. Look after yourself!"

Mr Tibbs the cat was accustomed to prowling back gardens. He could disappear easily since he was adept at climbing fences, and could thus reach the roof of the next-door garden shed and thence carefully down onto the access road behind or alternatively climb into the neighbour's apple tree. For a large greyhound, albeit one in prime physical condition and anxious to take on any challenge, escape was not so easy. Metre-high wooden fences were no problem to him, as he had already demonstrated – though he had to be careful he didn't vault straight into a rose bush on the other side. Painful! But the three adjoining gardens all had high rear walls with sturdy two-metre-high gates preventing any passer-by from gaining access. In his own garden, George had a gate that had an indoor handle...but

it was also bolted – he had done that himself earlier, not antici-
pating that he would turn into a greyhound. Now, no dog could
get in or out.

George bounced over to the next garden in line to inspect any
possible exit. No luck: try the next. Yes! At last a way out. The
back gate in this property was the stable-door sort, the bottom
half bolted shut, the top half slightly open. With a bit of encouragement, the top half could be swung right back and then with a
run and a jump George could leap over the bottom gate and thus
gain freedom. With an excited bark he was out!

The wide world beckoned. George shouted out goodbye to
his tabby friend, sitting now on top of the garden shed, and he
galloped down past the garages to where the access road
emerged onto the street. He was anxious to explore further afield
and exploit his newfound dogginess. It was still early morning
and most people he reckoned would still be having breakfast or
just setting off to work, so where might he join them?

The revenge he had just exacted upon Stephen Maxwell
opened up interesting possibilities. He was now, in all appearances and in the opinion of all dumb humans, just a stray dog on
the streets with no possible understanding of the ways of men
and women. This was an entirely liberating thought: he could
visit mayhem on whomsoever he chose, doing things as a
greyhound that he would never have the nerve to do as George
the respectable accountant. So – who and where next?

The answer was obvious – St Bartholomew's!

The college was about a couple of miles away but there was
no rush. It would be at least another hour before people were
moving about in large numbers so George had plenty of time to
wander along, down and through the village and eventually to
the fields at the other end that separated them from Durham city.
Meanwhile, he was intrigued by the olfactory sensation of just
passing by houses and gardens that he'd seen thousands of times
before but never knew they conveyed images to his nose that

were more colourful than the array of goodies in a confectionary shop window.

He stopped at one remarkably aromatic and diverting gatepost a hundred yards or so downhill from the terrace where he lived. He reckoned two or three brother dogs had visited this spot, though his nose was not so well-trained as yet to put a time upon it – maybe a day or even a week ago? His canine urges now got the better of him and he felt an irresistible impulse to leave his own particular scent in this highly attractive outpost – so he lifted a leg…just as the owner of the house emerged, coming down the front garden path with the resident hound: a big, heavy Alsatian.

The Alsatian erupted in a fit of barking just as George was dousing their exit route with his own distinctive brew. "Gerroff! Get away! This is my territory – I'll chase you to the ends of the earth and bite yer balls off!"

Alsatians were noisy dogs and George resented such aggression directed at him in a heavy Franco-German accent.

"You great hairy mutt!" he called back. "Who do you think you are barking at? You couldn't catch me even with a rocket stuck up your backside!" He bounded away a couple of yards, stopped and leered back at the Alsatian with his head on one side, his tongue lolling out the other and his eyes rolling insanely. It was the closest he could think of to blowing a raspberry but he had produced a dreadful, manic, unsettling grimace that came straight out of a rabid dog's worst nightmare. The Alsatian howled like a foghorn, broke away from his owner and rushed blindly at George as if he wanted to eliminate all memory of him. George cantered away at half speed, looking over his shoulder and laughing all the time. The madder his pursuer got, the more George laughed and the more he bounded out of reach; twenty-five yards of this and then George thought he'd give it full power – he wanted to know what he could manage if he really put his mind to it.

Greyhounds have the fasted acceleration of all animals on the planet, with the exception of cheetahs on the African savannah. They can reach speeds of over 40mph in a couple of seconds and George wondered if he could do it. For a middle-aged man with a paunch and no athletic background such speeds were only possible on four wheels and with a lot of horsepower under the bonnet, and even in his Land Rover he wouldn't be able to catch himself now. George was away like a bullet. Sheer exhilaration drove him on and the poor, overweight Alsatian came to a despairing halt, watching his persecutor dwindle into a speck in the distance. There was simply no contest.

Tearing along at high speed, George came to a crossroads and had to put the brakes on. He skidded around the house on the corner, claws scratching the pavement and he strained to realign himself to enter the side road without smacking into several parked cars that, despite his rapid deceleration, threatened to bring him to a dead, bone-crunching stop. Phew! He had to be careful he didn't get carried away with his newfound abilities.

He could hardly say that he didn't know the layout of the roads around here – but in his doggy excitement, and with a much lower eye-line, George was experiencing an entirely new world. As if to confirm that, the next sensation to assault his senses was the wonderful smell of fried sausages, egg and bacon. Super-sensitive nostrils were telling him that breakfast was cooking up. The utterly bewitching scent came wafting towards him from somewhere over the other side of the street and it drew him in like an angler reeling in a salmon. He hopped and leapt in delight, nose in the air, as he followed the tell-tale aroma towards a little detached bungalow opposite, sitting in a pretty garden with a yellow privet hedge fronting the pavement. A small wooden gate was half-open, inviting him in to this wonderful place.

The smell was strongest emanating from the rear of the bungalow. The garden stretched all around the property, so

George gambolled around with it until the lawn opened up at the back. There, at the head of the back garden, through open French windows he could see an older man seated at a table and watching the morning television news. He was obviously waiting for his fried breakfast, the bewitching scent of which was issuing from the kitchen behind him where presumably it was his wife wielding a large and extremely interesting frying pan.

George reckoned that good behaviour was the order of the day if he wanted to gain anything from this encounter. He trotted up quietly and sat down just outside the windows, looking in at the television. The morning news bulletin was showing. The anchorman was giving the latest report on a meeting of European Finance ministers and their views on the future economic prospects of the European Union. George could guess the outcome – disagreement on what policies should be implemented and when the anchorman gave his summing up, George uttered an annoyed "Wuff!" The stupid politicians could always be relied upon to do too little and too late. The politics of the EU were as overly cautious and exasperating as ever.

The man of the house looked quizzically across at his new four-footed companion, quietly sitting close by him and following every word of the television broadcast. He picked up the remote control and changed channels. George gave another annoyed "Wuff" and stared at the older man. He told him, in as clear as animal-speak could convey, that changing channels whilst he was absorbed in what the newsman was saying, was really a bit off. One doesn't do that sort of thing with one's guests. The older man got the message. He switched the channel back. George nodded his thanks and gave a friendly grunt.

The news now moved on to consider that evening's football match – a local derby between Newcastle United and Sunderland. Since half of George's office would be rooting for one team and the other half for the other, this was a news item of considerable interest to George: raised on the Tyne and a black and white supporter since he had first learned to sing *The Blaydon Races* as a child. He shuffled forward and peered intently at the TV set. Even the captivating smell of fried sausages could not distract him from the next few minutes of commentary.

"Elizabeth!" called out the man at the table. "Come and see the most remarkable pooch I have ever seen. Look: I swear he understands everything that is going-on on the box."

"Oh don't exaggerate, Geoffrey. He's just some dumb stray off the street. I don't know why you encourage them!"

George was rather put out by this remark. He thought of himself as a distinguished and elegant hound of aristocratic breeding. He looked back disparagingly at the lady of the house and told her just what he thought of that comment.

Geoffrey senior retorted, "There you go, Elizabeth. He knows what you said and thoroughly disagrees. Look at him. The most intelligent hound I have ever met."

George wuffed kindly at his host. Clearly the man was an educated and discriminating individual.

Elizabeth came closer to look at George. George stayed on his haunches but turned his head to give this woman the benefit of the best and most gracious smile he could summon up.

"Hmmm," she murmured, "I have to say he is not your average stray. He does have a look about him that I find…different."

George got to his feet and bowed. This woman may not have been quite as convinced as her husband as to his exceptional qualities but, whatever, she controlled access to the frying pan. A most important person to win over.

Geoffrey looked at his wife. Elizabeth looked back. This dog was certainly no ordinary animal – he really did seem to understand what was going on. The couple laughed.

"Elizabeth – you must go and put another sausage or two in the pan. We cannot let this creature leave us without some sort of reward!"

George gave an excited and most appreciative bark. If asked, he would gladly jump hoops for these two.

And so the next half hour was passed in a most agreeable and stomach-satisfying fashion. George was in need of rest and refreshment after his early-morning dash and this kind couple had shown no hesitation in sharing their breakfast with him. After demolishing the sausages and other leftovers they gave him, George offered to clean the plates that his hosts had served themselves. He licked them spotless. Then he nosed round the garden and picked a spot that was warm and comfortable in the rising sun so that he could lie down and have a sleep. He first thanked his hosts for their impeccable hospitality, and then he left them to go and stretch out and take a quick nap.

The last time George had gone to sleep he woke up a different animal so this time, as soon as he opened his eyes, he quickly looked down and checked himself. No change. He was still Greyhound George. Great! He was amused to find that he was actually glad about his continued dogginess. Accountancy could wait – for how long he did not know. What he did know, looking up at the sun and calculating its path across the sky, was that he must have been sleeping for about an hour, so now it was time he resumed his journey to St Bartholomew's College where he hoped to enjoy himself spreading a little chaos. He remembered a couple of times, many years ago now when he was a secondary schoolboy, that a dog had got into his school playground and scores of children had followed it around as if it was the Pied Piper of Hamlyn. No end of fun could be had like that, and he wondered if university students would react the same way. Nothing for it but to put his hypothesis to the test. He could not wait to become such a piper and put a similar plan into action. George stood up, stretched every leg in turn and then trotted out of the garden and into the main street leading down to the village centre. *St Bart's, here I come!*

Chapter 5

St Bartholomew's was one of Durham University's newer colleges, which is to say that for such a traditional and historic institution it was built in the 1960s – much later than many of the other buildings and departments – when the post-war surge in student numbers needed to be accommodated. Rather than stone, slate and a sombre, classical appearance like some of the older edifices, St Bart's was a brick-walled, pitched-tiled roof establishment constructed to form three quadrangles that bordered the university woodlands on the south-eastern edge of the city, on the hill that overlooked the spectacular Norman cathedral – one of Britain's finest architectural treasures. George approached the college from the east, leaving his own village, traversing across the River Wear, past a number of rugby and football pitches that led up to woodlands and thence, despite a myriad of fascinating scents en route, to the university property.

It was gone nine o'clock, George reckoned, but still there were some sleepy students dragging themselves out of their rooms, looking to catch a late breakfast. He followed a train of them into the main dining hall, located across a quadrangle from the residential quarters, to where numbers of students, kitchen staff and one or two college porters were milling about, going in and out. Upon entering the long, high-windowed hall, a table of young men was first to notice the inquisitive black greyhound and they called over in decidedly high spirits to see if it wanted to share their repast. That was exceedingly generous of them, George noted, and although he wasn't now that hungry he did not want to offend their hospitality. However, a member of the college domestic staff, a porter, alerted by the students' cries, tried to stop George trotting over to the table that had invited him. A chorus of objections issued forth.

"Shame, sir!"

"Leave off!"

"Let the poor dog through!"

"It looks like it needs a feed!"

Now George was a bit put out by this. A greyhound in form is not fat and, to be sure, its lower limbs are quite slim and its flanks and abdomen, to the untrained eye, are positively slender. But its chest, shoulders and back haunches are solid muscle and George's engine room, so to speak, was ready to explode into action at the slightest twitch. The implication that he was a poor creature in much need of sustenance could not go unchallenged. The attempt by some overweight college porter to try and stop his advance was all the excuse George needed. *Zing!* Like an arrow from a bow he flew past a flailing arm and was away down the hall, determined to impress his onlookers.

Unfortunately, a highly polished wooden floor set about with dining tables, chairs and various personnel moving around is not the ideal arena for a bit of Olympian racing. And it is far too slippery to show off your abilities at slalom. Crash! George gave an empty chair a glancing blow. Over-compensating, he skidded next into someone's legs – at the speed he was going he noticed only denim jeans and had no idea of gender – except that they were well-padded and he bounced off them into a nearby table. Krump! *Ouch! That hurt!* The table didn't move much but George's right shoulder had taken a fierce blow and now, what was this white cloth wrapped around his head as he slewed to a halt? A tablecloth? The crashing and smashing of crockery and the spilling of cereals, juice and other items of food and drink all over the floor confirmed that, yes, a tablecloth was indeed what it was. From a table stacked full of breakfast provisions.

Pandemonium ensued. People were laughing, shouting, trying to get out of the way; trying to tidy up what had fallen; someone was calling for a mop; someone else was trying to get hold of George; George meanwhile was limping with a bruised shoulder towards another table and trying to avoid capture.

One of the kitchen ladies was carrying a tray full of used plates and breakfast bowls, piloting a path as best she could between the carnage, and she suddenly jumped in surprise as George popped out from behind a couple of chairs that barred his passage. The poor woman stepped quickly back but slipped on a puddle of spilt water behind her. Crash! Down went the tray of crockery, some plates wheeling off to all quarters.

A great cheer went up. George quickly ducked out of sight again. Another tablecloth obstructed his passage and there was nothing for it now but to keep ploughing on in the attempt to put distance between him and his pursuers. There was a slipping and sliding noise behind him as the tablecloth was pulled and then Sper-lash! – several jugs of orange juice and packets of cereals came toppling down, spilling their contents all over the place.

The college porter hurried forward, swearing at the scene of disaster. He caught sight of George at first, but George was not staying put and waiting for retribution. He scampered off from one table to another across the hall. The students, of course, loved it.

"Hooray!"

"There it goes!"

"Tally Ho!"

"Where's that damned dog gone?" swore the college porter, trying not to tread on any of the mess scattered about.

Rather belatedly, George regretted what he had started. But more than regret, he felt it was time to, er, disappear. He needed to put as much distance as he could between him and someone who wanted to get hold of him and make him pay for the turmoil he had inflicted upon the college. There were around twenty or so students in various locations about the dining hall and George reckoned his chances of escape were better if he plotted a zigzag route around them – trusting that none would want to grab hold of him with such determination as the porter he was trying to evade. Adrenalin was putting a hold on the pain from his shoulder so he skipped out from behind the table he was under, trotted quickly behind a couple seated a few yards away, turned past another student, under another table and drew a bead on some open double doors at the opposite end of the hall from where he had entered. The porter saw him, lunged across but with another surge of excitement George dashed away, heading for freedom. A cheer sounded out behind him as he made the doors. The young men who had first called out to George were now applauding his supercharged exit from their company.

More careful this time, George put the anchor down as soon as he passed out of the dining hall and into the passageway outside. It was just as well he did because there – coming towards him, summoned by the chaos that he had caused and, spread across, blocking the way he wanted to go – was his wife Annabel, armed with a mop and accompanied by a couple of other cleaning ladies.

Aaargh! What to do? A quick about-turn would have wrenched George's injured shoulder too much so there was no alternative now but to go plunging straight ahead into the three women.

George had on occasions thought about visiting his wife at work but had always resisted the impulse. It wasn't too difficult. He knew that as senior housekeeper in the college, Annabel was in charge of cleaning student rooms and communal areas and she had a team of mostly ladies who were armed with mops, brooms and a variety of other materials to help them in their task. Annabel wielded a mop like she wielded a whip and no disorderly environment could survive her onslaught. George knew only too well the impact of her influence at home where she exercised only a fraction of her considerable potential; he had no interest whatsoever in seeing her at work in college where her talents could be given full rein. But now, confronted by this all-powerful Amazon, this enemy of all-known germs, this human Domestos, George the unstoppable force of chaos, confusion and spilt breakfasts was running full tilt into the most immovable of all objects.

One of the three women squealed. Then whoosh! The mop came hissing down in a vicious arc, aimed at and just missing George's head. George barked angrily, showing his teeth, and darted for the gap between his wife and the woman next to her. It was all show on his part – there was no way he wanted to bite anyone, let alone his own nearest and dearest, but the moment of hesitation and apprehension on the part of those in front of him was all he needed. With another burst of acceleration he barged his way through and was away, down the passageway, round the corner at the end, and now thankfully out of sight.

But he was not yet free. George was still inside a large, rectangular college building, where one passage led into another and there was no outer door open that he could find to let him into the college grounds and back into the woodlands. The first door he encountered was shut and it was the sort with a round doorknob you needed to turn to open. No good to a creature without hands. George kept going, hoping that the passage he was following would not lead to locked doors at the end. And he was limping badly now; his shoulder was beginning to hurt.

In the distance behind he could hear noises: people were coming after him. It sounded like the porter, the cleaning ladies and several laughing students. Annabel would be sure to be with them, undoubtedly angry and wielding her mop or some other weapon. George really did not relish another confrontation. He hurried on…but where to? He emitted a small howl of concern.

Round the next corner he could see a succession of offices and two large, heavy oaken doors at the end which undoubtedly led outside and to freedom. Except that they were shut and, again, featured round, brass doorknobs. Useless. Where could he go? Discarding all other possible escape routes as inaccessible, he found one door immediately to his left that sported a handle. The plaque in the centre of this door read: Student Welfare Officer.

George wondered if this officer would welcome a doggy visitor. He pawed the handle – it moved down and opened. He limped gratefully inside and, wonder of wonders, the office was empty. If he could now just shut the door behind him he should evade detection. George pressed his backside into reverse, the door yielded and he heard it click shut. Safe! He'd found this bolt-hole just as a number of people could be heard moving outside down the corridor he had just vacated. The buzz of noise that moved with them went past his door. Various sounds of surprise could then be heard when the dog-hunters reached the end of the passageway, opened the outside doors and found neither sight nor sound of their canine quarry anywhere.

George relaxed at last. There was a desk, two chairs on either side, and a sofa beside a filing cabinet in this small office. The air was undisturbed, quiet and peaceful – just what he was looking for. He climbed onto the sofa for a rest.

Greyhounds are the sort of predators who, like cheetahs, rely on sudden acceleration to catch their prey, and although capable of immense speeds they quickly tire. Once they've caught and eaten their dinner they will then settle down and sleep for long periods. Not for no reason are they known as 40mph couch potatoes. George had earlier not known much about this remarkable breed of animal, but he was learning about them in a very personal way now. The excitement of the chase was over, he was comfortable in his new surroundings, his bruised body was supported by foam rubber and his long legs were happy, dangling a little over the edge of the sofa. Within a few moments, he was fast asleep.

Time passed. George had absolutely no idea how long he had been out, but he was raised back into consciousness by a wet tongue licking his face.

George blinked. His head was a bit foggy but he recognised that tongue.

"Hello, Rosie," he muttered sleepily.

"Well, goodness, George, this *is* a surprise!"

George came-to very quickly. He looked up. There was Rosie the greyhound inches away from his face; there was her owner, tracksuited Carol, looking down upon him in what could only be described as amused fascination bordering upon hilarity, and there he was stretched out in all his gangling splendour over a rather confining sofa. In his pyjamas.

George looked at himself. He had returned to human form.

"I know I asked you to come and meet me after work some day this week, George, but I didn't quite expect to find you so soon and here, in my office, like this. What's this? Some sort of invitation? A girl could get quite the wrong idea from your style of dress."

George blustered. He swung his legs round and clutched his pyjamas alarmingly about him as he sat up. No way he wanted his rather loose and unbuttoned night attire to reveal anything of his anatomy beneath.

"Er, excuse me...I was fast asleep..."

"I gathered that, George. But why here? This is a little forward of you, don't you think? I mean we don't know each other that well as yet, do we? Or do we?" Carol smiled teasingly.

"No, no, sorry. Sssh! I'm not supposed to be here...I dunno how this happened!" George was mortified to find himself in this state of affairs closeted away with this highly attractive female explosive and with his own spouse and goodness knows how many other witnesses nearby in the immediate proximity.

"Well, I'm sure *I* don't know how this happened either. But I am pleased to see you coming out of your shell, George. And I suppose I should be quite flattered by your advances...though expressed in a somewhat idiosyncratic manner, I have to say."

"Nothing of the sort...er...I was sleepwalking." George was searching his brain for something to explain his sudden appearance in this office. Anything, except for the bizarre truth.

Carol looked at him with amused scepticism: she clearly

didn't believe a word of it. Rosie the greyhound resumed licking his face, however. She needed no explanation.

"Now, now, George, you live *miles* away. We both know that. You can't have walked all the way from there in your sleep. Good try but you'll have to do better than that."

George waved Rosie back. "No, really. I was, er, spending the night in one of the student rooms, I mean the guest rooms, above here and the next thing I know…here I am."

This was a bit more plausible. The college's residential quarters always kept a number of rooms available for invited speakers, foreign visitors and honoured guests. Carol peered at George quizzically. Was this the truth?

"Oh yes? I'll just call the housekeeper and check which room…" She reached for the phone on the desk.

"No!" George clambered to his feet in alarm. "Don't phone my wife! Please!"

Carol's eyes opened wide. "The housekeeper? Of course – Annabel Potts. So she's your *wife*! Well I would never have guessed. Oh, George, whatever are you doing? Married to the Dragon of all people!"

"The Dragon?"

"That's what the students call her. The fiercest individual on the campus – and you are married to her. Well, well, well, that just about explains everything. No wonder you don't sleep at home!"

"I *do*! Of course I do! Well, that is, I was here last night of course. But that was just a one-off. Now I really need to get back home." George stopped. There was a problem there – how on earth was he going to get back to his village in his present pyjamaed appearance?

George Potts, second accountant to Durham City Council and a conservative, respectable and trustworthy member of the community pulled himself together and tried to strike a pose of upstanding solemnity and esteem in the room of the Student

Welfare Officer of St Bartholomew's College – admittedly a trifle difficult in a crumpled, blue-striped sleep-suit with a greyhound nosing his private parts. But he made a decent attempt of it.

"Ahem, young lady, I wonder if you would be so good as to offer me a lift home in your motor? It seems I have got myself lost here and it would not do to be seen strolling about in this establishment in my current state of, er, undress. I am indeed very sorry to trouble you but I fear that neither mine own reputation, nor that of this of this distinguished university institution, would be enhanced by the sight of me, like this, in this place..." George dropped a hand to stop Rosie invading his pyjama bottoms.

Carol smiled at him. She was absolutely sure she had not garnered the correct explanation for the appearance of this man in her office, dressed as he was for bed, but she was certain also that she could not drag any more out of him without offending his dignity. She would not yet prick the bubble of self-esteem that he was struggling to create in her presence. Instead, she reached for the phone.

"Don't!" George pleaded, his face a masque of horror.

"It's not the Dragon, don't worry! I'm calling for the car," Carol whispered back.

"Hello, Sally? Can you talk? Yes? Great. Can you come over in the car and pick me up? Yes, and pick up a rather unexpected visitor of mine, too. Who? None other than George Potts. Yes. But he looks a bit different from when we saw him last...Mmm..."

George grimaced and turned away. He couldn't leave the room but he didn't want to hear any more. He could see this was going to be a major topic of conversation between these two irrepressible female friends for ages to come. He was never going to be able to forget this, ever, he could see that. Meanwhile the phone conversation was continuing, whether he liked it or not. He fondled Rosie's head while he waited for the interminable and embarrassing telephonic interchange to come to an end.

"Mmm, Sally, I know. Amazing! Well I was out walking Rosie as I usually do when I've got a minute spare and, lo and behold, when I get back I'm confronted by this long, striped something or other stretched out on my office sofa. What? Yes. Unbelievable. You've seen those old wartime photos of concentration camp survivors in striped pyjamas, haven't you? Yes. Something like that. About as starved but a bit more spirited though. Denies he was trying anything on. I don't believe him but anyway I think we ought to take him home and put him to bed. What do you think? Yes. Can you come? Great, Thanks. See you. Bye!"

"Really, Carol, that's a bit rich," George protested, "comparing me to some poor, starving concentration camp inmate. You and your friend – you go a bit far sometimes!"

Carol turned back to face her guest. "Don't you dare complain, George, we're going to try and save your bacon. If I can get you out of here without anyone noticing, that is. And as for reputations, we'll just have to wait and see what happens." She laughed. "I did say there was something of the wild side about you when we first met, didn't I? You're not *really* an accountant, are you?"

Chapter 6

Sally, a research associate in the Department of Psychology just above the woodlands that bordered St Bart's, took only five minutes bringing the car round. She hurried straight away into Carol's office, dying to see the spectacle on show. She was not disappointed.

"Oh, George, what a picture!" she hooted.

George was resigned to this by now. "Any other friends you want to invite round to revel in my embarrassment?" he asked sarcastically.

"I hadn't thought of any more," said Carol, "but we'll find others if you're up for it."

George shuddered. "Please, no! Just get me home, quickly."

"So what's he doing here, Carol?" Sally asked, intrigued. "Going to a pyjama party?"

"Dunno, Sal. He's being very evasive about that...though he claims to be married to one of our staff on these premises and you'll never guess who..."

"Who? Tell me."

"Our housekeeper – you know her, don't you?"

"What? The Dragon? I do *not* believe it! I didn't think anyone could survive being hitched to her for long!"

"Do you mind? You are talking about the woman with whom I have been, er, happily married for decades. Do you have absolutely no regard for my feelings?"

"Well yes, we do, George," said Carol, "though I'm surprised if you've any sensibilities left at all if you've been living with her all this time. I can barely breathe after working in this college with her for only a couple of terms!"

George could understand this. His wife was not the easiest of persons to live with but he was damned if he would concede an iota of this in front of these two ebullient tormentors.

"Look, leave off, will you? Are you just going to stand around enjoying my discomfort or are you going to help get me out of here? I do not want anyone, least of all my wife, seeing me here in this state."

"OK, George," Carol laughed. "We'll spirit you out of here as best we can – anyone outside, do you know, Sal?"

Sally peeped outside along the corridor. "Nope, the coast is clear. C'mon, George, the car is right outside."

With Sally in the lead, George in the middle, Carol guarding the rear and Rosie quite clearly enjoying all the fuss and hovering around all three of them, the party shimmied out from the office, along the few yards to the main exit, and then across a short tarmac area to the car park and the waiting red mini. Sally had to open the passenger door and put the seat up to allow George and Rosie access to the rear of the two-door car and while she was doing this someone called out from a short distance away by the side of the college building.

"Excuse me! Miss Davies! Wait up a second!"

George recognised the voice and froze in discomfort. It was the college porter who not so long ago was trying to catch him under the tables of the dining hall.

Carol turned and waited for the porter to approach.

"Hello, Barry. Anything I can do to help?"

Barry the porter drew near and as he did so gave a quick glance at George, a stooping beanstalk of a middle-aged man, dressed in blue-striped pyjamas and about to accompany a large sandy-coloured dog into the rear of a small red car. A master of self-control, if this was anything out of the ordinary to pass in a Durham University establishment, Barry gave absolutely no indication of it. Obviously he had seen quite a few strange things in his many years on the campus. *What discipline; what a man,* Carol thought.

"Miss Davies, you don't know anything about a large black greyhound racing around this college, do you? Is that animal one of yours?"

Carol laughed innocently. "No, Barry, nothing to do with me. Here's Rosie, with me as always. I'd never let her get away from me whilst at work, you know that. Oh, by the way, let me introduce you to Dr Potts, a visiting professor of psychology who is engaged in some very interesting experiments here. Dr Potts – this is Barry, one of the dearest members of the domestic staff we have at St Bart's."

Inside the car, George could hear Sally give off a fizzing sound at this introduction but he decided to ignore this and held himself up very straight and dignified, as different as possible, he thought, from anything remotely dog-like. He extended a pyjamaed arm to Barry the porter and shook his hand warmly. "Ahem! Pleased to meet you," he said briskly.

"So what's this about a black greyhound, Barry?" Carol was intrigued. She was the only owner of such a breed of dog in the vicinity, so far as she knew.

"Some crazy dog that went crashing through the dining hall like a rocket, Miss. Dunno where it came from, nor where it went but it caused any amount of damage, I can tell you." Barry scratched his head, puzzled by it all. "The housekeeper was furious; the kitchen staff were in a right pansy about it; 'course the students enjoyed it all. No bloody help to any of us, they were. I reckon one of 'em must have spirited it into the place and then gone and hidden it after. But if you ever find out who's got that dog, let me know will you? Strictly against college rules, in't it? I mean, you are the exception like, Miss. We all accept that...so long as your dog don't go on the rampage like this one did..."

"No fear of that, Barry. Really. I don't want Rosie to cause any sort of trouble at St Bart's and to be honest, bless her, she wouldn't want to either. But thanks for telling me. I'll keep a close eye out for this other one. Bye now!"

Rosie and George were now safely battened down on the back

seat of the mini, so Carol got into the front. Sally started up and they set off along the college drive, downhill and onto the main road out of town. Sally was still chortling at what Carol had said.

"Visiting professor of psychology! Hah! That's a good one!"

"Did you see Barry? Tell him that it's only a professor wandering around in pyjamas and he didn't blink an eye," grinned Carol in reply. "It just goes to show what ordinary folk think of us academics. They reckon we're all crazy!"

"Quite right too," said George, not quite sure if he should be glad of, or feel insulted by the subterfuge foisted upon him. "Being entirely normal myself I felt extremely uncomfortable being caught out in the open like this, but clearly for university people like yourselves, outrageous behaviour and forms of dress are perfectly acceptable." He snorted disparagingly. George had never been to university and had got on in life only by dint of hard work and whatever luck was going. He felt somewhat intimidated by all these over-confident, highfalutin academics with scores of letters after their names – his two female chaperones included.

Carol ignored this remark. Her mind had now turned to the message that Barry the porter had delivered to her. A wild greyhound had been on the loose at St Bartholomew's and, if this continued, she guessed it would not be long before the authorities turned up the heat on people like herself who bent the rules. She could bring in Rosie to work on the odd day or two so long as no one officially complained and, of course, the students who came to see her never did. Everyone loved her hound. But a dog rampaging about in college, particularly a greyhound, was a direct threat to her and Rosie's welfare. Carol wondered what had happened whilst she had been off the premises that morning, walking her own greyhound. She decided to ask her visitor: one who had indeed been guilty of some decidedly odd conduct that very same morning.

"George, you didn't hear or see anything of this black

greyhound charging around the college before I found you, did you?"

George visibly shrunk at the suggestion. "Certainly not," he replied shiftily. "Nothing whatsoever to do with me!"

Carol looked at Sally, who looked quickly back whilst negotiating a roundabout. Both thought the same. There was something not quite right in that voice. George was hiding something.

"Oh ho!" cried Carol. "Out with it, George! You know something!"

"Indeed I do not! You are a highly suspicious, distrustful and reprehensible member of the female class. You insult me, you threaten me, you doubt my word and you make disparaging remarks about my partner in life...I do not know what I have done to deserve you. You should be ashamed of yourself – intimidating decent, honest pillars of the local community like myself."

"Yes, yes, yes, so you say, George. Now stop evading the point. You're as guilty as sin. We both can smell it! What were you up to this morning, letting strange dogs loose?"

"I do not know what you are talking about. I never released any dog, any animal whatsoever in the college this morning."

"Sally, do you believe him?"

"No!"

"Neither do I. George – we don't believe you. Cough it up! What were you doing? Where were you immediately before I discovered you in my office this morning?"

"Nowhere! Doing nothing! Leave off, will you? I'm innocent! I saw no other dog this morning. Honest!"

George was fidgeting in his seat in alarm, trying to stroke Rosie but his own restlessness was disturbing his canine companion, quite apart from signalling his own guilty involvement in unspecified goings-on that morning.

"George, if you do not own up straight away to what mischief you've been perpetrating then Sally will stop this car and we will haul you out onto the pavement and grill you in the street – in your pyjamas and in front of half the commuters travelling into this city. So come on! Spill the beans."

"I've nothing to spill! I've told you – I'm innocent; I am falsely accused."

"Sally!"

Sally hit the brakes and the mini skidded to a halt. Carol opened the door, climbed out and pulled the seat forward.

"Out you get, George!" she commanded.

"No! This is ridiculous. I can't get out like this!"

"Oh yes you can! You certainly can't stay there. Neither Sally nor I will share this car with a liar and a scoundrel and an instigator of canine chaos in St Bart's. I won't even let Rosie near you again, even though she seems love-struck with you so far. So – out you get!"

"Please, Carol – get back in the car. Look – you are causing a traffic jam behind!"

"Are you going to tell me what you've been up to?"

"Aargh! OK! Later. Not now. I can't here. When you get me home. Please – I've got to go home and change. Get back in the car!"

Sally looked round. "Is that a faithful, honest-to-goodness promise, George? That you'll tell us all when we get you home?"

George scowled. "Yes!" he groaned. "Get me home and I'll tell you what I know..." He was blowed if he would tell them all, though.

Carol wasn't entirely convinced and her body language conveyed that impression. George looked out of the car at her, standing there on the pavement, frowning with her hands on hips and her body curved away from him in doubt and disbelief. She was wearing that figure-hugging tracksuit again and looking absolutely gorgeous – enough to melt a heart of steel. George couldn't utter another syllable. If he tried he would just burble

incoherently. He directed his gaze back down at Rosie and trans-
ferred his attentions to stroking her head. He didn't trust himself
to look at that siren, summoning him to his disaster.

Carol got slowly back into the car, staring at George who
refused to meet her eyes. She didn't believe him for a second.
Sally started up again and the car drew away from the kerb,
heading towards George's village. It was only five minutes ride
away. Five minutes of George sitting in sullen silence and the
two women wondering what was going on in his mind.

George directed them to park at the back of the house, as before.
He knew he had a problem getting back in to his home and the
only way he could do so with involving a minimum of attention
from his neighbours was to vault over the garden fences in the
same manner as he left. He realised of course that, if noticed, a
dog leaping over garden fences would probably cause fewer
eyebrows to raise than seeing George Potts doing the same in his
pyjamas, but there was nothing for it – if he wanted to recover
his keys, a-vaulting he had to go.

How was he to explain his actions to his companions now?
Well he wouldn't, that's all. Jumping over a neighbour's imitation
stable door he would demonstrate as the normal way he went
home and there was nothing more to be said about it. Except that
a decidedly unfit and uncoordinated fifty-something year old
was nowhere near adept at surmounting doors and fences as a
racing greyhound in tip-top condition. Trying to haul himself up
the bottom half of the stable door, straddling it and then
swinging his legs over, all the time trying to protect his modesty
and prevent his pyjama bottoms from gaping apart and
revealing all, was a complex combination of manoeuvres that
was exceedingly trying and almost beyond him. It *was* beyond
him. His female audience was reduced to fits of laughter.

"I cannot believe what I am seeing," gasped Sally in between
shrieks of merriment.

"George, do not deny that you've ever been in a circus – this is first-class entertainment," Carol applauded. "You really are the king of clowns!"

With a final flourish George got both legs across the lower half of the stable door, pirouetted around and slid down into the garden beyond, all the time trying to maintain a dignified expression as if this was the sort of thing he did all the time. Except of course that, disturbed by all the noise and encouragement from two delighted onlookers in the access lane outside, Mrs Catherine Forsyth – neighbour and owner of the property he was entering – appeared hurrying down the garden path to greet George just as his blue-pyjamaed frame plopped down on the back lawn in front of her.

"Um, good morning, Mr Potts. Nice of you to drop in like this… Any particular reason for your visit?" Mrs Forsyth had travelled the world a bit in her youth and had been through riots and earthquakes before. She was determined that the sudden and unexpected visit of the man from next-door-but-one would not upset her, even if he appeared to be in the process of ripping off his pyjamas as he did so.

"So sorry to bother you, Mrs Forsyth. Didn't want to cause a fuss, see, but I've locked myself out, ha! ha! Came out the back in my pyjamas, as you can tell, but the gate slammed shut on me. Silly, I know. Do you mind if I climb over your fence now?" George was sidling over in the direction of his own garden as he said all this. He nodded apologetically to his neighbour as he lifted one leg over the fence and then the other.

Mrs Forsyth nodded in return: "Go ahead, Mr Potts. Please don't let me stop you." She observed that one trouser leg became caught on a fence post as he was doing this and ripped apart.

"Oops! Oh dear," remarked George. "Never mind, can't stop…" He waved a grateful goodbye to his neighbour, hopped across the next garden and then dragged himself over the last remaining barrier before reaching safety amongst a host of

Annabel's standard roses. Rose thorns invading his person then felt a blessed relief after the stings and arrows of misfortune he had felt ever since waking up in Carol's office in utterly inappropriate attire earlier that day. He was home at last!

George made his way up the back garden to the plot by the dustbin where he had buried the keys. Scrabbling in the dirt he quickly found them and then opened up the back gate to let his two young women companions enter. He ignored their generous, joyous, not to mention tearful salute of his gymnastic endeavours and led them and Rosie – meanwhile clutching pyjama trousers about his nether regions with one hand – to the back door, which he promptly unlocked to let them all inside. Finally he suggested his guests make themselves at home, excused himself, and then scurried as quickly as decorum allowed upstairs to shower and change.

Twenty minutes later he was back in their company, offering tea and biscuits.

"No thanks, George," Carol replied. "Very kind of you but we'd rather not inconvenience you or ourselves. We prefer nosing around your place first to see if it confirms what we think of you."

Various rooms and facilities were entered and examined, accompanied by occasional disapproving noises, exclamations and shaking of heads. George ignored all and went for his study draw. He drew out his hipflask and shook it. Nothing inside. *Damn!* He collapsed onto his desk chair. Rosie found him first, followed shortly by Carol and Sally.

"Well, this is more like it!" Sally volunteered, entering the study. "At last a place of anarchy and interest."

"A refuge amongst all the iron orderliness and discipline," Carol surmised. "This has to be your study, George, and I bet you wage a battle with your other half to keep it this way."

George didn't say a word. These women had him all sized up. The two young females took a quick tour of the study, then

Carol said, "C'mon, Sally, let's go upstairs now!"

George protested weakly. He knew the two were running all over him but he couldn't stop them. This was an unwarranted intrusion into his private life and he could have thrown them out if he wanted to, but there was a sort of desperation in this house that had been slowly accumulating over the years, something now he realised he was ashamed of but he suddenly had no defences. Intimate details of his life were being revealed and he couldn't stop it. Masochistically, he didn't want to stop it. He did not fully realise this yet but if he seriously didn't like where he was in his life right now then he had to suffer the shame and embarrassment of having it all revealed to critical outsiders before he could find a way to reverse direction and, returning back to zero, start rebuilding his life again. He sat there, frozen for the time being and gloomily awaiting the outcome of this house search.

"Oh no!"

George heard a plaintive cry from above. He refused to move, remaining rooted in his study chair.

"Oh, George!"

Another cry. Then a clattering of feet downstairs as they came down to confront him. Carol entered his study first and, again, George did not want to face her. But he had to.

It was Sally, however, who spoke up. "Two single beds, George! Not much opportunity for sexual adventures there! What a comment that makes about personal relationships..."

"So don't comment. Please don't!" George just sat there with a wooden expression on his face. He was facing two attractive, extrovert and highly sensual women and couldn't help comparing them to the one with whom he had chosen to spend the rest of his life. Suddenly he felt as miserable as sin.

Carol uttered not a word but her face said it all. Sadness written all over it.

Magical Rosie came forward and licked George's hand as if in consolation. She knew too. Being married to the Dragon was no fun.

There was a cold, stony silence for a few seconds and the two women looked at each other as George lowered his head. Then Carol changed the subject. Away from the subject that none of them actually wanted to mention.

"Right, George, now we've got you here...time to tell us about this morning. You promised you would. So what were you doing at St Bart's and how did this involve a black greyhound?"

George saw an opportunity to use the depressed silence they were all anxious to avoid as a cover for his early-morning antics.

"Um, erm, I said I'd seen no other dog earlier today...that was not, er, strictly true. I *did* see a black greyhound in college before I got to your office, Carol..."

"Aha! Now the criminal speaks. What were you doing there, eh? And has this dog got anything to do with you wandering about in pyjamas?"

"My sleeping arrangements, my movements about in pyjamas and my relations with my wife are a private matter and I absolutely refuse to discuss those with you. I did, however, meet up with a spectacularly handsome and fit black greyhound and did encourage him to show off somewhat." George rubbed his shoulder at this point as the memory of a certain painful collision returned to him. He could still feel the bruising.

"And?"

"And so this remarkable creature did indeed dash about like lightning in a box and spread, erm, a certain amount of confusion about him. He went out of the dining hall and down the corridor towards your office, Carol, where I lost him – to go I know not where. And I didn't know it was *your* office, Carol, when I entered it. I was tired and looking for a place to rest, and the door announced that this was the office of the Student Welfare Officer, that's all. I had no idea that that was you."

In recounting all this, George made himself sound as sincere as possible – not too difficult since that story was not so very far from the truth.

"George – are you making this all up as you go along?" Carol peered at him, her beautiful eyes searching his own. George's own eyes flared up in return as he struggled to control his feelings but he held her gaze just long enough to confirm he was telling the truth. Not all the truth, but enough to make his account sufficiently credible.

"No, I'm not making this up. I'm telling you exactly what happened." He had to look away. Electricity began to sizzle between them; George's temperature was rising and he was beginning to sweat. *God*, he thought, *this is killing me! I've got to get this woman out of this place and away from me as soon as possible or I won't be responsible for my actions...*

Carol saw his eyes looking at her and she hurriedly turned her attention to her friend. "What do you think, Sally? Is he on the level?"

Sally could see George's reddening face and had no wish to prolong his agony and sexual frustration any further. "Yeah," she said. "I think he's telling the truth this time. Let him go!"

George huffed and sat up in his chair. He shook his head as if trying to clear his brain and get a grip on his emotions.

He decided to return to combative mode. "Let *me* go? Am I your prisoner now? Can I remind you that you are currently sitting in my home and it is *I* that shall let *you* go. And please go as far away from here and as quickly as possible now, thank you very much! I have had a very trying morning and am in need of peace, quiet and recuperation which you hyperactive two very clearly have no inkling of how to create."

Carol grinned as George's spirit rose and as he went for them on the attack. This was an altogether healthier note to leave him on. She replied in kind, "You are an ungrateful beast, George. Sally and I have saved your bacon this morning and have even left you with an excellent alibi if anyone asks of Barry who was that strange fellow wandering about in pyjamas this morning. We *will* leave you now – I've got a number of students and a pile of paperwork waiting for me in my office that you interrupted earlier – but don't think you are getting rid of us for long. In fact, give me your mobile number. We shall be back to save your life at some time in the future. You are our project to work on, remember. You have two professional psychologists here just itching to release you from your self-inflicted chains!"

"*Save* my life? Plague it more likely!" George rose to the bait. But he gave Carol his number and, after another less than subtle reminder, he graciously thanked her for organising her act of rescue. He wouldn't admit it but he secretly relished the thought of seeing her again – no matter if she and her friend were the most dangerous and disturbing influences he had ever met in his entire life before. Like sirens singing to him from the distance, he was irresistibly drawn towards them, and he knew that, for better or worse, his life was on the cusp of momentous change.

Chapter 7

George was in a very subdued mood that Monday evening when his wife returned home. She, of course, came blustering in from work barely able to contain her fury at what had transpired during the day – an uninvited alien visitor somehow appearing and disappearing in her ordered environment, *her* college, knocking over all and sundry and upsetting the established routine. George pretended to listen and put on a face of shocked concern as his wife vented her anger but he couldn't keep it up for long. He thought of trying to deflect her attention as soon as she drew breath in her tirade.

"Have you been watering the patio plants recently, dear? The weather's been hotting up of late. I seem to remember Stephen Maxwell saying a little while back that they need some attention. Does he mean re-potting?"

Annabel Potts stopped in surprise. Her husband showing some interest in gardening? And he was right to be concerned about the patio plants, too – a fair bit of maintenance was necessary with them to prepare for the summer. She really ought to go seek advice from her neighbour.

"Do you know, I think they might! Thank you, George. So good of you to show an interest at last. I'll have to ask Stevie to pop around and look at them this weekend and see what he recommends. You can never be too careful. I don't want to lose any of my beauties…"

George cringed. She spoke of her plants as if they were her pets, as if they had feelings of their own – whereas he knew that any cat or dog in the neighbourhood she would gratefully string up, if given half a chance. And now he'd gone and given her an excuse to have Smarmy Stephen around to visit. He couldn't stomach that – he'd have to go out for the day.

"Yes, dear," he agreed. He was racking his brains to think of an excuse to disappear for as long as possible on Saturday or Sunday. Then an idea occurred to him.

"Why don't you ask him to come over on Saturday? I've got to go in to Durham that morning to examine the university's plans to buy up some council property, so I can get out of your hair and leave you two to the garden. What do you think?"

It was as good a ruse as any. The university's expansion plans had been talked about for the last year at least and there was still a lot of talking to be done before the project got underway. George could stay out under that pretence for as long as he liked. If the weather was good he would like that very much. A long walk out in the countryside beckoned.

It was decided. Annabel spent the next half hour on the phone, clucking like a contented hen with Smarmy Stephen and arranging a gardening get-together for the weekend, leaving George in his study, solemnly reflecting on the eventful day that he had had and what it all signified.

George's self-esteem had hit a low point. The contrasting emotions, and bodily forms, he had been through that day had brought him finally to wonder where he was and what he had achieved in his life. Not much, he concluded. The experience of dashing around as a greyhound had pointed out all that he had not done as a man. He was not a dashing sort of fellow, after all. And the sad fact was, he rather preferred being a dog! George wondered idly what concatenation of events had led to him to wake up as a super-fit, black greyhound. He wondered also, if he wasn't careful somehow, whether or not it would happen again. Equally, if it did, and given the most embarrassing consequences of his later return to human form, he puzzled over whether he might actually be able to control his metamorphoses. If so, all sorts of wild possibilities lay before him. He rather liked that idea. Ensconced in his study, locked into his own thoughts, George found himself most unexpectedly envying a dog's life rather than that of a fully grown man.

Nothing much happened to him over the next few days, however. George returned to routine at work, apologising for his absence on Monday where he truthfully recounted that he really couldn't explain exactly what had come over him, only that he wasn't feeling his usual self that day. Completely out of sorts, he said. He ventured the notion that maybe he had picked up some sort of malarial illness – you know, those bugs that invade your system and that you can never quite quit: they flare up now and again and lay you low unexpectedly for a while. Had he ever been to the tropics? Well no, but he had met any number of people who had and maybe it was catching?

It was only one day off, of course, and his colleagues were not really put out that much. No medical note was requested. It was just George, being a bit idiosyncratic as always and as we all have a right to be – but he was always as regular and reliable and about as full of surprises as an old clock. So it was back to work as before and life in the office maintained its efficient progress with hardly a hiccup such that by Friday, if anyone had asked, no one would have remembered that George had been anywhere else but at his desk all week.

Then, at one pm whilst he was just delving into his packed lunch, George's mobile rang. It was Carol.

"Hello, Professor, you old rascal, are you in your night wear today? Or is the experiment concluded?"

George spluttered over his ham and cheese sandwich. He looked round hastily. The office was half–empty with those in the nearest workstations away in the canteen. He nonetheless kept his voice down.

"There was never any experiment – that was your own crazy idea," he whispered.

"It was *your* crazy idea to appear in college in pyjamas!"

George didn't want to get into that topic of conversation. "Yes, yes, nice of you to remind me. What do you want? I'm busy at work at the moment."

"Really? Lion taming, is it? High-wire act? How many other clowns with you?"

"Ha, ha. Very funny. Now suppose you tell me why you called…"

"Well actually, George, Sally and I have been talking…" (*I bet they have,* thought George, *they probably haven't stopped talking all week.*) "…and we've decided to take you out this weekend. Give you a run, so to speak, with Rosie. We are going up to a beach on the Northumberland coast, and we are taking a picnic, and we thought that this was just the occasion to invite you to come along. Get you out and liberate you. Shake the dust off you that's been accumulating for decades. So you have to come. It's decided."

"Very kind of you for thinking of me, Carol, but I do *not* need liberating. You and your friend, on the other hand, need to be locked up, kept off the streets and prevented from ruining other people's lives. Especially mine."

"George, that is most ungrateful of you. If you remember correctly it was *you* that was on the verge of ruin last time we met and it was *we* who rescued you. Now I come to think of it, I should have just left you to your own devices on Monday; let you run the gauntlet of trying to get out of college without the housekeeper or any of her staff seeing you."

"Ooof!" George shivered.

Carol smiled. She still didn't know what he had been up to that morning, wandering around St Bart's in his pyjamas, but it didn't matter. She'd struck home with that gibe.

"Come out with us, George. You know you have to."

She was right. He couldn't resist. But George wasn't giving way without a fight.

"Young lady, you are the most sadistic torturess I have ever encountered and I flatly refuse to go anywhere with you, at any time, *unless*…" George paused for effect and to get his listener's full attention, "…unless you promise to behave properly and not insult, upset or otherwise offend my company. If you do so promise, I might *just* accept your offer of a picnic with Rosie. She at least is a responsible companion."

There was burst of cackling down the line. George surmised that both Carol and Sally were listening in to his reply. He was not similarly amused

"I'm waiting for an answer."

"Yes, George, we both promise, don't we, Sal?" Carol couldn't stop laughing. "We love you to bits really."

Oh yeah, thought George. They could promise away until they were blue in the face but he knew it didn't mean anything. They would continue to make his life uncomfortable, whatever he did or said or tried to arrange. He knew he would have to put up with whatever they threw at him. He was actually quite flattered that they wanted to see him, no matter if it was only to see him writhe in agony at their expense.

"As it happens, I was going out for a walk on my own tomorrow morning anyway, so if it's a picnic with you tomorrow it's a deal. Not on Sunday, however. I shall need a day to get over you, I'm sure."

More laughter down the phone. However, arrangements were concluded: George would meet his escorts in town at 9.30 am and they would conduct him, as before with Rosie in the back of the mini, an hour or so's journey up to Northumberland to embrace its magnificent coastline.

Saturday morning dawned bright and cheerful and George couldn't wait to finish breakfast and prepare himself for his day's excursion. He told Annabel that he would lunch out and probably go for a walk in the afternoon if his business concluded satisfactorily before then. He hoped she would enjoy herself gardening and busying about at home after the troublesome week she had had at work. Annabel said thank you, she certainly planned to enjoy herself, that George should do too and he was not to hurry back on her account – though would he call so she could get tea ready? Of course! Everything was *so* jolly between them. Maybe his married life wasn't a prison sentence after all?

George left the house ridiculously early and, with an hour before his scheduled meeting time, he decided to walk into Durham rather than take his motor. He would still have plenty of time to stop at the supermarket en route and buy some provisions for the picnic – come to think of it, since he would not be driving he could take the opportunity to indulge in his favourite tipple: malt whisky. Yes – an excellent plan.

When Sally and Carol found him, George was walking along somewhat absent-mindedly with a carrier bag in his hand and a slow smile spreading across his face. As he climbed across to the rear seat of the mini, his carrier bag gave out a revealing clink and…and was there the smell of alcohol on his breath?

"George, have you been drinking *already*?" Carol looked at him accusingly.

"Me? Would I ever? Hello, Rosie, old girl. Lovely to make your acquaintance again…"

"George, this is simply disgraceful. If you've started boozing already then what are you going to be like later in the day? I have no intention of sharing a picnic with a drunken old sot!"

"Shall we kick him out before we start, Carol?" Sally joined in.

George settled himself in the back of the mini and arranged Rosie's head on his lap. He looked up and grinned at the two women who were scowling at him. This was going to be an entertaining day, he could feel it already. He made a point of not attempting to move a muscle.

"Ladies, please forgive me but the thought of spending the next few hours in your company did in fact drive me to drink. Only a small tot, please be assured, but a necessary precaution given what I am undoubtedly going to suffer at your hands. If you can restrain yourselves in my presence however, and refrain from making me a constant source of your amusement then I shall not resort to the bottle every couple of minutes. Indeed, I might even learn to enjoy your friendship...OK?"

Carol elaborately turned her back on him and sat down. "Agreed," she snorted. "It's a truce...for now."

George smiled to himself. *Round one to me,* he thought. "Come on, Sally," he cried out, "get moving – we've got a long way to go."

The two girls looked at one another as Sally put the car in gear and they accelerated away. They couldn't help a slight grin at each other too.

Saturday mornings, the main roads in and around Newcastle were busy so the mini took a little longer than anticipated to get clear of the conurbation and strike out north in the direction of the coast. They wandered a little, looking for byways that were not clogged with parked cars and searching for a side road that would take them to an appropriately deserted beach where they could spread themselves out and relax in the sun. It was gone eleven am when they finally arrived at their destination, and it was getting hot too. By the time they had found the spot they wanted, George was itching to free his long legs from the back seat of the car and go off on a walk over the sand dunes. He took Rosie and left the girls to sort out the blankets and the various bags of food and drink they had brought for the picnic.

"See you in half an hour, ladies," George called out mischievously as he escaped up the nearest dune. "Behave yourselves and keep off the whisky!"

The sun was rising; as he topped the first bank the breeze was in his face and there was not a cloud on George's horizon. His spirits rose and they were not alcoholic spirits. George plodded on towards the sea then came down off the sand dunes and onto a firm expanse of beach that the receding tide was spreading out in front of him. There was no one else around. He let Rosie off her leash and watched her go bounding off at top speed, only to come pattering to a halt some fifty yards away, then turn and come cantering back, her mouth open and smiling, her tongue out, her eyes shining at him in the sun.

Yes, George thought, *enjoy it, Rosie. This is the life – I almost wish I could join you!* He had to shake his head free of such thoughts, however. He had to make the most of what he had and not wish for any other life. As it happened, he thought, look where he was and who he was with now. Not such a bad set up at all. He just had to keep his emotions tightly under control every time he looked at Carol and her friend. He swore they became more alluring and attractive every time he saw them and Carol in particular had a way of arousing his hormones that was especially discomforting. Was it obvious? He tried not to think of her. She was more dangerous to his mental health than a barrel of malt whisky.

Rosie was bouncing around him and what with the glorious weather, his desire to empty his thoughts and this affectionate greyhound encouraging him, George almost broke into a gallop himself. What was becoming of him – this dog and her owner were certainly brightening up his life. He looked around and when he was sure there was no one else in sight he did allow himself a little run. It didn't last long however – he was soon out of puff. Bent over and with his chest heaving he decided that that was enough of exercise – it was time to return to the picnic and his two female escorts.

George laboured his way back up over the sand dunes to where he and Rosie had started out. It was a bit of a sun trap between the dunes where the sea breeze couldn't reach and that was why he came stumbling in surprise upon two languorous lovelies stretched out on blankets and both wearing, if that was how it could be described, the briefest of swimwear.

He collapsed down in a heap on a patch as far away as possible from them.

"Heavens above, girls, this is too much! Too much flesh entirely. I might be an old man but I'm not yet altogether past it and what you are doing to my blood pressure looking like that is positively murderous. Where's the bottle?" George dived into the nearest bag.

Carol twisted several acres of terrifying nakedness around and glared at him. "Don't you dare, George! If it's blood pressure that's bothering you then downing that whisky will only make it worse. And don't be such an old fossil. Sally and I are only sunbathing."

"Yes, George, don't worry," Sally piped up. "This is not an invitation to an orgy. You can keep your trousers on!"

"Good God!" George saw another yard of flesh turning towards him. He hurriedly looked away and fished out a plastic cup to accompany his bottle. He splashed out three fingers of Ardbeg, 10-year-old Islay, and glugged it down.

"Aah!"

Sacrilege, he thought, *swigging this stuff back and barely tasting it.* But his immediate need for semi-comatose dizziness was greater than his desire to appreciate the finer points of Scotland's greatest export. George sank back, staring skywards. He reached for something, anything, to cover his eyes.

Carol looked at him. *He is a darling,* she thought. *But utterly hopeless.* She thought better than to tell him that he was at that very moment blindly fumbling with several items of her discarded clothing to place over his head.

George meanwhile was quickly shutting the lights out and attempting to switch off consciousness as a means of regaining some modicum of composure in the presence of these two fatally irresistible goddesses. He focused on savouring the last drops of malt whisky that remained on his tongue – a much safer direction of thoughts than to consider what lay outside just a few feet away. Then he felt Rosie come down and nuzzle beside him. Good grief! That could not help but be disturbing in his present hypersensitive state – a warm body too close which only reminded him of two other warm bodies nearby. He groaned aloud. What was going on? Even his nostrils seemed to be full of the aroma of femininity; he really must get a grip...*O blessed darkness...swallow me up,* he prayed.

It seemed like only seconds later when George felt Rosie's nose exploring his face. She licked him. George kept his eyes shut. *Not yet,* he thought, *let me doze a bit longer yet.*

Then he felt Rosie examining another part of his anatomy altogether. That was too much – his masculine parts. He quickly told Rosie to lay off – this was an altogether unwarranted intrusion into his personal belongings.

Feeling somewhat put out, George grumpily came round to see two bikini-clad beauties staring down at him – their features expressing surprise, concern, even amazement. He wasn't sure what.

"Are you seeing what I'm seeing, Sally," asked Carol, "or am I dreaming?"

"Nope. I'm seeing the same."

"And are you thinking what I'm thinking?"

"Yep, I think so"

"It *is* George, isn't it?"

"Dunno"

"George in disguise?"

"It's a very *good* disguise..."

Greyhound George jumped up. Rosie was again sniffing his hind quarters in great interest.

"Rosie! Gerrof! I won't tell you again – that is inadmissible evidence!" George was quite firm – in his dog-speak, that is. Rosie whimpered and backed off, quite hurt.

"I say," said Carol, "he's quite argumentative, isn't he? Poor Rosie!"

"That fits," said Sally. "It's got to be George."

Carol stooped over, showing a good part of her boobs. "Are you George?" she enquired of this big, white-bibbed, black greyhound.

George wasn't sure where to look, or how to react, given this provocation. He did his best not to blush.

"If you're George," Sally volunteered, "stand on your back legs and clap your front paws!"

George gave her a withering look and held his nose in the air. He was not some performing goon in a circus. He barked "NO!" in a most forceful manner and shook his head.

Both girls laughed.

"I don't think he liked that request, Sal," said Carol.

Carol looked at George again. "If you *are* George, then prove it to us somehow…"

George couldn't stop goggling at those glorious golden globes that were now being upended in front of him. He might be a dog at this moment but he realised his human and masculine sensibilities were still very much present in his loins. He wanted to put his head in the sand – in fact he looked round at the nearest dune and promptly did so.

"What *is* he up to?" wondered Sally.

"I haven't the faintest idea." Carol looked similarly perplexed.

Of course not, thought George, half buried in sand dune. *Women never have a bloody clue as to what they do to us males.* But when he had cooled down sufficiently, he returned to face his audience and then he drew a line in the sand. At least it looked like a line in the sand to the two girls until this marvellous creature started drawing others. In front of their startled eyes, this is what they saw the greyhound drawing out:

I'M GEOR…

He couldn't finish. The two girls shouted out simultaneously: "It's *George*!"

George stood aside from his artwork and graciously lowered his head. He bowed doggily. His two admirers clapped excitedly.

"Oh, George, I just *knew* there was something wild about you!" Carol was in ecstasy. "And no wonder Rosie felt that too! How long have you been, er, shape-changing like this?"

George shrugged his shoulders. How to answer this? He trotted over and scratched out his last effort and then drew:

2 WEEKS?

Sally and Carol looked at each other and both immediately started talking animatedly about what this latest signal meant. Two weeks? Why, that meant dog and man had only been changing one into the other since they had got to know him! And the mysterious greyhound at St Bart's was George, all along! How fabulous! The pyjamas still needed explaining away but they would surely get to the bottom of that soon enough and wasn't all this *so* exciting...

George soon got fed up with this. Why did women have to go into a gaggle and talk about everything and examine every single little detail of everybody else's lives? He wouldn't stay here listening to this gossip any longer. He was off!

As before, George was exhilarated by the explosive power of his own musculature. Boom! It didn't matter that the sand dunes tried to slip and slide under his pounding feet – his touch was so rapid that he was up and over them and down on to the beach the other side in a matter of seconds. He streaked like a rifle bullet in a straight line for the sea, his spine flexing and springing back to lend extra power to his long legs. In the time it took for his female admirers to realise he'd gone, he was splashing about contentedly in the waves. Bliss!

A few seconds passed before Rosie caught up with him .She wanted to play as well. George felt a little guilty at his treatment of Rosie. He was one of her kind now, after all. He splashed over.

"Sorry, Rosie," he called out. "Sorry if I was a bit short with you just then but you know it takes a bit of getting used to – these sudden changes I go through."

Rosie's big eyes looked at him reproachfully. She had always been quite a quiet animal, a dog of few words, as George now realised. He apologised again.

"Don't look at me like that. I said I'm sorry…"

"OK," Rosie replied slowly. "Just don't snap at me again…"

Oh bloody hell, thought George, *this one's a* very *sensitive female. However am I going to cope with all these different women?* He came over and touched noses – hoping to show he wasn't such a heartless macho after all.

Rosie licked him back. She was clearly interested in him. This was a puzzle for George and he had simply to figure this out as soon as possible – was he a man or dog? He walked around Rosie as she walked around him. What was he *feeling*?

George noticed the two girls running towards them as he did this. What was he feeling about them as well? He didn't get much chance to decide before Carol launched into him.

"George! Now behave yourself! I know what dogs do and it looks like you've started doing it. So stop! Right now!"

George stopped and sat on his haunches, holding his head on one side as he looked quizzically at Rosie's owner. What was she getting all heated about?

"Don't you look at me as if you don't know what I'm talking about. You behave, hear me? The fact is, whatever you look like at the moment, I can't help but think of you as a lovable though cantankerous man of mature years who I positively adore…and I will not have an old dog like you mounting my beautiful bitch. Do you hear? No way! That would be positively *bestial*…not to mention the biological consequences would be quite unpredictable, indeed unthinkable. So lay off her! Bad dog! Bad man! Bad whatever!"

George laughed. He looked at Rosie. She wasn't laughing, poor Rosie.

George got up and looked at the two women who were now standing before him. Yes…he still felt decidedly human as soon as he looked at their long, luscious bronze limbs which, from his lowdown point of view, seemed to lead unerringly to the Place of No Return. He broke out in a sweat and then gave voice to his feelings in as unmistakeable way as he could. He told Carol that her sandy-coloured hound was safe from his advances – here he apologised yet again to Rosie – *but just be careful with how you dress yourselves and how you handle me! I'm still a spirited and hot-blooded male whether in a somewhat worn and frayed human body or in that of a racing greyhound in his prime!* He barked it out as urgently as he could – and then dashed into the nearby surf to cool off.

Rosie and the two semi-clad goddesses looked at him.

"Did you get that, Carol?" Sally asked.

"Not sure, Sal" she replied. "He certainly knew what *I* was talking about. I *think* he was saying what he's been saying all along. You know: 'Leave off and let me alone,' like. As if he can look after himself…which of course we know he can't"

Sally and Carol both looked thoughtful, watching Greyhound George prance about in the waves. This was quite an experience – a relationship which was very much a first for them both; for anyone, indeed.

"Tell you what, Carol," said Sally, "this has got to be the most challenging case study in psychology that anyone, anywhere has ever faced."

"Mmm," agreed Carol, "it would make our fortunes and earn us professorships if we could ever make any sense of it. Not that anyone would believe us…"

Greyhound George raced past, doing his best to splash the two of them.

Chapter 8

It was time to eat. George was feeling famished, what with a sudden change of metabolism and a lot of running in and out of the waves. He trotted off in the direction of where they had set out the picnic and trusted that the others would follow. Of course they did – all three females were drawn to him like a magnet. George turned his head to look back at them as he topped the first dune – this was an extremely satisfying and confidence-boosting experience. He had never had pretty females – of any species – running after him in his life before. *Yep,* he thought, *a dog's life ain't so bad.*

Approaching the picnic blanket he saw a number of seagulls circling around and dropping down to examine the unattended store of food. What a bloody nerve! Typical opportunists on the look-out for what they could steal, he thought. He was down there in an instant, snapping his jaws at the closest.

A chorus of squawking erupted as he leapt perilously close at one or two birds. A wild flapping of wings carried them all away, however, before he could do any damage.

"Hey! Keep off, you big brute," one screamed at him with a distinctive naval accent. "Plenty enough food here for everyone, don't you be so greedy!"

"You'll be food for me if you get any closer!" George retorted. He wondered if seagulls tasted anything like chicken. Possibly. With his speed of attack he'd nearly got one – but then reckoned it would most probably be a mouthful of feathers that would be all he'd get. He flopped down on the blanket and looked at them, wheeling above and crying out in frustration at being denied their goal. *Funny,* he thought. *One minute I'm feeling distinctively human urges; the next I'm being decidedly doggy and trying to catch seagulls.* A confusing psyche; though he guessed matters would resolve themselves in time.

Meanwhile, where was the food? He put his nose into the first bag. A variety of packed meats, cheeses, bread and fruit assaulted his senses. No wonder those seagulls were interested. He guessed animal olfactory senses were more attuned to food than humans. He knew only too well what his human senses were attuned to in present company. Best to forget that. He turned his attention to a particularly attractive package of cold meat. Oooh! It practically stood up and talked to him. *Oh dear,* he thought, *I hope those girls hurry up. It wouldn't do to start ripping open packages before they get here.* He could imagine their reaction.

Rosie came first, soon followed by the two girls: all delightfully leggy creatures. *Stop thinking like that!* George opened his jaws and let his tongue hang out. He didn't know what, or who, he wanted to eat first.

"George is hungry for something," Sally remarked, sitting down with a bag at her feet.

Too right, thought George. *Oh dear! I've really got to control myself!*

"Here, George, try a frankfurter while we unwrap the rest." Sally proffered a waving wand of processed meat in his direction. George took the sausage delicately in his teeth, carefully avoiding contact with the fingers that held it, then tossed it into the air and caught it with a clack of his jaws as gravity returned it to him.

"Bravo!" cried Sally.

"You old show-off, George," laughed Carol.

George champed the sausage down and looked at her, his eyes twinkling. *Well,* he tried to explain, *I've got to exercise my senses of coordination, my new complex anatomy.* It was thoroughly rejuvenating, finding himself in a highly responsive, super-fit body – albeit one of canine inheritance.

The meal passed extremely pleasantly – the two girls fussing over the two greyhounds, especially one of them: their new, unexpectedly transformed guest. For George, he relaxed totally.

There was no longer the battle of the sexes going on – he didn't have to be on his mettle every second, retorting to every gibe they threw at him. In fact, in his doggy form, he was able to lap up the evident affection they felt for him as they acquainted themselves with an unthreatening, generally co-operative and really quite handsome greyhound that could not answer back.

A bowl of water was put down for the two dogs to share. George looked mournfully up at his providers. *Nothing else?*

Carol waved a finger at him. "If you think we're putting whisky down for you, you can think again!" she warned. "Your bodyweight index is way below what it was when you were human so you'll get drunk even quicker."

George yapped in disagreement.

"Don't try and argue," she smiled. "I know your internal digestive system must have got used to the quantities of alcohol you abused it with as a man...but you've got a different body now. Besides," and here Carol rammed on the whisky cork as hard as she could, "with no hands, no chance now!"

George barked in annoyance. This was taking unfair advantage!

Rosie crept up to him. "What is it with humans and alcohol, George? Every time they go near it I see them behaving stupidly. And the stuff tastes foul – you surely don't like it, do you?"

George didn't feel he could quite explain to Rosie the peculiar attraction of 10-year-old Ardbeg. He did concede that Rosie was right about a lot of drinkers and their stupid behaviour. Especially in the market place at night, after pub closing time. What he wondered about, and now was denied the experimental evidence to resolve the issue, was whether it tasted as sublime to his canine taste buds as it had done just a few hours earlier to his human palate when he couldn't resist the temptation for a quick nip whilst he was waiting for the mini to pick him up. George grumped again about this and shot a foul glance at Carol close beside him. The progress of scientific investigation was again being set back by the tiny-minded, overly practical and protective instincts of women compared, he thought, to the adventurous curiosity of menfolk who had a more abstract, theoretical and altogether wider interest in the laws that governed the universe.

George clambered to his feet. He had one woman at home who strove daily to confine his ambit as a man. And here was Carol insisting on doing the same when he was a dog. That was enough! It was time for George to exercise his rights as a free animal; as a dog off the leash; as an honest inquirer into the boundaries of science, the extent of his own canine capabilities, and the particular limits of these sand dunes. Having eaten and drunk his fill, well – that which he had been allowed – he would now up and off and go exploring. The leggy lovelies, all three of them, could do whatever they damn well wanted.

"Hello?" said Sally. "Where's he off to now?" She noticed a determined look about his gait as George strode off and up the nearest dune

"Better pack these things away, Sal," said Carol. "We'll have to follow. Who knows what sort of mischief he'll get into now he's like this. Rosie!" she ordered. "You get after him first and keep an eye on what he's up to until we get there."

A frenzy of packing followed as the girls put everything back into bags, picked up their clothes, the blankets, assorted bottles of sun cream and oils and hurriedly stowed it all back in the car. They each pulled something over their tops before setting off after the dogs – they had no idea where they going now, whether it be into the sea or up inland. They agreed that George could be perfectly bloody-minded if it suited him.

George, as it happened, was sniffing out rabbits amongst the dunes. He had seen a movement and cantered over to inspect – only to find the creature concerned had bolted as soon as he had seen him coming. That was a challenge if ever he saw one! George ran across to inspect where his quarry had been – and there were the tell-tale droppings of rabbit, and marks leading away to a hole in the ground.

The next twenty minutes were taken by George finding one hole, then another and then more: a regular warren that extended some distance north along the coast and inland towards some golf links. Try as he might, however, he could not catch any rabbits. He could hear some movement down one tunnel and he even shouted down to ask if whatever was in there would like to come out and play. But he got no takers.

Rosie found him, snuffling around one opening. "I'm afraid it's no use, George," she said. "I've seen these rabbit warrens before. You can't get in and they'll never come out if they can smell you here."

George nodded. Like with Mr Tibbs, the tabby cat at home who never believed him at first, no rabbit was going to risk coming out into the open and play the sort of games that hounds normally get up to with smaller mammals.

"Yeah – I guess you're right," he said. "Come on – let's see what other fun can be had." He trotted off in the direction of the golf links.

From atop the nearest dune a narrow road could be seen in the distance, rising and falling down towards them from the main A1 highway, heading for the coast. It came to an end not so far from where the two dogs stood – the road leading into a fenced-off clubhouse. The gate which marked the entry to the clubhouse and the end of the road also spawned a couple of footpaths that led further in their direction. One went onto the golf course proper; the other one led straight towards the beach, bisecting the links with the green of the fourth hole on one side and the tee for the fifth on the other. There were people moving across from the fourth to the fifth hole while George was looking. This deserved some investigation.

Before he could move, however, Carol called out: "Wait up, George!" The girls were coming.

He didn't wait. George left Rosie behind and went ahead to reach the footpath where it opened onto the beach. He started jogging up it towards the golf course, passing a notice on the way that read:

EMBLEFORD GOLF COURSE. *Private Property. No access beyond the public footpath. Keep all dogs on a lead.*

This he ignored and kept going. George arrived to find a dozen or so people dotted around various places on the golf course, and in particular he noticed a large, round and expensively tailored man at that moment carting a golf bag across the path towards the fifth tee, followed by a second man of slighter and smaller build, also wheeling his golf cart, but not so ostentatiously attired.

The bigger of the two men – fat, self-important and overdressed – swore at the black greyhound that he saw approaching. He was the sort that has all the most expensive gear available: from his fancy flamboyant hat, down past his voluminous plus-fours to his large, spotless and unnecessarily-fringed golf shoes. He was the sort that thought putting on a show was the whole point about playing golf. He was the sort that George took an instant dislike to.

The fat man looked round and caught sight of Carol and Sally who were now coming up the path from the beach, following George. Rosie was with them and walking on a lead. Clearly in a bad mood, the fat man called out: "Hey! Can't you read? Get your dog here under control – put him on a lead!"

This had the same effect on Carol as it did on George. She waited until she had walked up closer and did not need to shout, then she gave a sly wink at George and replied, "That, sir, is *not* my dog. My dog is with me, and as you can see, she is on a lead and very well-behaved. But I've never seen *him*," here she pointed at George who was bouncing nearby with a grin on his face, "in my life before today, so if you want to get him under control, do it yourself!"

This was as much encouragement as George needed. He first galloped a wide circle around the fat man, yelping and whining and trying to act as the sort of friendly dog that wanted to play. Then at the irate call of: "Shoo! Get away! Go on!" George came loping up onto the fifth tee, looking at the fat man as innocently as a young pup. He sat down close by, put his head on one side and waited, looking as amicable and cooperative and harmless as could be. Carol and Sally walked on a few paces up the footpath and then stopped to see what would happen next. They knew perfectly well that George was planning something.

The fat man and his smaller companion had a little conversation where clearly they decided to ignore their various spectators and to continue playing. The larger, dominant one placed his ball on a tee, drew out a club from his golf bag and then shaped up to take a swing.

The black greyhound let out an enormous sneeze.

The fat man nearly fell over as he tried not to hit the ball. In fact, in swinging his club around and missing, he described a neat pirouette, nearly decapitated his colleague behind him and succeeded only in screwing his feet into the ground. Various colourful epithets followed, directed at Greyhound George, who only looked back as innocently as ever.

The fat man teed up again and, before starting his swing this time, he pointed his club at George and warned him in a low, threatening voice: "You villainous pooch – if you so much as uttered a sound again you'll get this round your head!"

George didn't twitch. He just sat there, smiling as well as any dog can, and looking as innocent as a babe. *About as innocent as dynamite on a short fuse,* thought Carol. Meanwhile, the man took aim and hastily brought his club arcing down as quickly as he could before any other interruption could prevent it.

The golf ball whistled away into the blue and, as luck would have it, it seemed to be going in a straight line towards the distant flag, though perhaps it was not going quite so far as the fat golfer would have preferred. George went whistling away too, his elastic frame flying over the turf, his piercing eyes locked onto the little white ball where it dropped out of the heavens and bounced onto the fairway. To the consternation of the golfer, George caught the ball while it was still bouncing – a really neat bit of speed, skill and quick jaws – whereupon he did a quick about-turn to come racing back to where he started. Then George trotted up to the fat man and deposited the ball at his feet.

Carol and Sally both clapped enthusiastically.

"Isn't he a good dog?" cried Sally. "Look! He went off to fetch the man's ball for him."

"Wasn't that *clever*!" agreed Carol.

The air about the fifth tee exploded with a vocabulary that was really quite inventive, George thought as he retreated a safe distance from the man and his golf club. Then the fat man turned and looked at the girls as if he wanted to strangle their lovely necks. "The ball shouldn't be touched," he spluttered. "It's not supposed to be returned to me!"

"Oh, isn't it?" Carol asked, playing the dumb bimbo. "You don't want to lose it, surely!"

This sent the fat man off into further colourful paroxysms. He banged his club from one podgy hand to another and darted looks of pure hostility first at George and then at the two girls.

"Don't you know anything about golf, you idiot!" the fat man cursed. "I'm aiming for that flag!" He pointed at the fifth hole in the distance, his face reddening, his feet stamping on the ground.

Carol ventured the opinion to Sally that perhaps it was not only dogs that should be put on leads and kept under control on this golf course.

After a pause to allow time for his colleague to calm down, the smaller man eventually took his turn to tee off. George had returned to sitting and spectating again – only a little further away this time – and he now watched the next ball to go flying down the fairway. He didn't move.

The fat man glared at the girls and then walked in George's direction, shouting at him and trying to get him to go away. George politely retreated out of range, still with a look of innocence about him, and when the man and his threats receded, he then moved back to where he had been before.

Bang! Again the fat man drove off. Whoosh! As soon as the ball was in the air, away went George accelerating even faster than before as if driven by the voluble curses that were being hurled in his direction. Yet again George caught the ball before it had come to rest but this time off he went racing into the distance towards the flag on the fifth hole. He came scrabbling to a halt and, lowering his head, he promptly dropped the ball as close to the hole as he could. He then sat back on his haunches and looked at the four people at the tee who were watching him. He gave a triumphant bark.

"Oh bravo!" Sally applauded.

"What an intelligent animal!" cried Carol at the fat golfer. "Look – he understood what you were trying to do and he's helping you."

"Aaagh!" The fat man threw his club into the bag and, swearing like a carpenter who has just hammered his thumb, off he stomped down the fairway, refusing to look at the girls and yanking his golf cart behind him.

"I say!" said Carol loudly at the man's disappearing back. "You'd think he'd be a bit more grateful to dumb animals, don't you reckon?"

Sally tried to control a fit of giggling.

The smaller man left behind on the tee started packing away his club and tried hard not to smirk as he prepared to follow after his unfortunate partner. Carol and Sally waved goodbye as he set off.

"Do thank your bad-tempered friend for the giving us such entertainment," Carol called out.

"We *have* enjoyed this afternoon," agreed Sally. "We do hope you will too."

The smaller man turned to look back and wave in return. He wore a broad smile across his face.

"Well that one's a gentleman at least," said Carol to her friend. They recommenced walking up the footpath, Rosie dutifully coming with them. In the distance, before he left the fifth hole and before his overweight adversary could reach him, George cocked a leg and watered the flag, the green and the little white golf ball that rested just a few inches from its destination. Then he bounded away into the sand dunes and disappeared.

It was some fifteen minutes later when all four met up again at the red mini. The girls and Rosie were waiting for him and as soon as they saw George swaggering his way back down the dunes towards them they burst into fits of laughter.

"George, you old rogue, that was simply magnificent. Don't try and tell us you've never been a clown in a circus!" Carol bent down to give him a hug; George promptly licked her nose.

"We knew all along there was a wild creature inside you," said Sally. "It just needed the doggy side of your personality to let it out!"

One way or the other there was much celebration at what had transpired. The girls were profuse in their praise of George's antics, and he was really quite pleased with himself for dreaming up some original retribution for an individual who had been exceedingly offensive and obnoxious to his escorts, quite apart from the threats made to his own canine person. Rosie came round to nuzzle up and quietly add her own congratulations.

Lapping up adulation from all sides was something that George thought he could quite get used to. It wasn't something he had previously been familiar with, so he indulged in it thoroughly while he could get it. He held his head in the air, closed his eyes and enjoyed the petting and nuzzling like a Hollywood lothario or a sultan in his harem. George even got to wondering if he might ever experience such a luxury in a bedchamber of his own. Then he was given the command to get into the car.

"That's enough of that, George," Carol ordered, "standing there like some Egyptian dog-god. Now we're going to shut you in the car while Sally and I change out of our beach wear. Avert your eyes like a good man – or dog! "

And in such ways does bliss become bathos. *The problem with becoming four-legged,* George realised, *is that people treat you as if you are a dumb animal. They are happy to pet and fawn all over you if that is how they feel at the time, but the next minute you are mere decoration; an inferior; a lesser being to be told what to do, ordered about, expected to jump through hoops, even.* Locked away in the mini, George gave vent to his feelings in no uncertain manner.

Half hidden behind a sand dune and hearing the commotion he was causing, Carol raised a head into his line of sight. "It's no use complaining, George," she called out to him. "What's a girl to do with a lively beast like you about? It's not like we don't trust you while we're stripping off..."

Here Sally's head popped up. "But we don't trust you!"

Both girls started laughing again.

George sank back grumpily onto the car seat. He couldn't clamber across to the front and work his large paws around the door catch that would ensure his freedom, so there was nothing to do but wait. And waiting for women to dress and arrange their affairs can take for ever, he realised. He was still sulking several long minutes later when the doors opened and his two female consorts, continuing in high spirits, climbed into the mini.

As Sally started up and turned the car round to drive off, Carol looked back over to her subdued passenger. She thought she recognised what he was feeling. The psychologist in her was getting into top gear just as the car was.

"I don't think he was happy, Sal – us shutting him up in here and depriving him of his liberty for so long. We cut him off in his prime for ten minutes or more and so he won't forgive us. D'you know what? The problem is that George's mind is still the same as it was but now he finds it in a youthful and athletic body. Naturally he wants to dash about in a rejuvenated fashion and do all the things that he never allowed himself to do when he was younger and in training to be a respectable, well-behaved and thoroughly expurgated accountant. Like spy on us in the buff, for example."

That was an unjust gibe: George wuffed in protest. Not that anyone took notice.

"Well, I should think he should be jolly grateful, in that case. I mean, I know he's a dog, but how many other middle-aged men get that chance? There's no reason just to sit there with a long face and look all sour and moody."

"I don't think he can help the long face, Sal."

"No. Perhaps not. But cheer up, George – we didn't lock you up for long!"

They were at it again – talking about him when he had no chance of reply. He growled and fidgeted about on the back seat as if he wanted to jump out of the car and run off. But of course, he couldn't; he just had to settle back and put up with the long drive home while his companions chattered about him interminably.

Chapter 9

Entering Durham, the girls parked a short distance away from St Bartholomew's College in the quiet road outside the little terrace house that they rented. They had left that morning with one greyhound and returned with two and, now they were back home, were not quite sure what to do with their guest. George took advantage of this indecision to have a quick look around – after all, he reasoned, these two unpredictable females knew where he lived; it was only fair that their abode become known to a volatile quadruped.

"He's rather a nosey beast, isn't he?" remarked Sally, after George had run up and down stairs, in and out of bed and bathrooms and had inspected the lounge, kitchen and had looked out the rear window at the tiny back yard.

"Yes – it's a wonder he hasn't opened the wardrobes in both bedrooms and played around with all our underwear. You know what some old men are like…"

George stopped immediately and glared at Carol in annoyance. Had she no respect? He pranced outside in a huff. There was nothing for it now but to remove himself from this place and find his way back to his own home. He greatly regretted leaving the bottle of single malt whisky behind and he barked at the girls to ensure that they knew it was his property and that he expected to come back for it someday and find it undisturbed. Well, that was his meaning – whether or not they understood, he could not say.

George said a fond goodbye to Rosie. He said he hoped she understood that their friendship could only be platonic and that he regretted he was too capricious a being to offer her a stable and meaningful relationship. He nonetheless would return to see her sometime, either in canine or human form, and would always value her company. Then with a last bark of cheerio he set off home.

It took him less time trotting as a greyhound to return that it did walking out earlier in the day as an ordinary pedestrian. As he eventually found himself back in his home village, the problem George was now confronted with was that he had had no means of calling his wife in advance; he carried no keys to enter his house and even if he could gain entry somehow it was going to be difficult to persuade his nearest and dearest that he was indeed her spouse and, yes, he did live there.

Such thoughts troubled George's mind as he turned the last corner before home. What was he to do? Well, the front door was no use. It would be locked, of course, and the doorbell was too high for him to reach. He stopped outside his front room window and tried to peer in. Nothing. Annabel's net curtains prevented any inquisitive passer-by, man or dog, from seeing anything. Better try round the back. Off George went to the access lane which led to the row of garden gates at the rear of each property. Again, frustration reigned – all the back garden gates were shut tight, even the stable door of the Forsyths, two doors down. What was a greyhound to do?

Then he heard a sound above in the apple tree between his garden and that of Smarmy Stephen. It was a miaow!

"Hello, is that you, George?" Mr Tibbs cautiously called. He wasn't in the habit of being friendly with dogs.

"Yeah. Am I glad to see you, Tibbs. I'm stuck here and I want to get in to my back garden."

"Dunno if I can help, pal. All the ways-in I know need decent, retractable claws to climb up. Dogs don't have 'em. You'd be better off changing back to a man."

"Can't control that, I'm afraid. But can you see if my wife – that's Annabel – is in the house? Maybe we can call her somehow?"

"Nah! She ain't in. I saw her leave some time ago. She's in with Smarmy Stephen now, and when she's in there she don't leave. Not for some time, anyway."

"Oh yes?"

"Yeah. Happens regularly whenever you ain't around. Didn't you know?" Mr Tibbs looked down at the puzzled face of the black greyhound. "Sorry if this news to you, an' all, but I'm always here, prowling around like, and I see it often."

Of course he would. Mr Tibbs was a regular visitor and spectator along these gardens, as George well knew. He must have the inside story on all the houses along this street, including his own. So...a regular liaison between Smarmy Stephen and Annabel, eh? George wasn't too surprised. How did he feel about that? He wasn't too sure...but now he was absolutely determined to get inside the back garden and see if he could see for himself.

"You OK, George? Not too shocked, like?"

"No, I'm OK, thanks, Tibbs. Good of you to ask. But I *am* getting angry...as if I want to batter the gate down."

"Don't try it, mate. Solid wood – you'll get hurt!"

George had an idea. He had deliberately left his own back gate unbolted – he must have subconsciously known that some such occasion as this might occur – so it would open if someone could depress the door handle on the inside. He wondered if Mr Tibbs could do it – a difficult manoeuvre, but he was a very resourceful cat.

"Tibbs, old chum, I wonder if you could help..." George explained what was necessary.

His tabby friend understood right away what was needed and George sat back and watched appreciatively as his furry accomplice set to work. Tibbs carefully dropped down out of the tree onto the neighbour's garden shed and from there tiptoed along the back wall then across to his own back gate. Poised directly above the door handle, George watched Tibbs slowly slide his top half down out of sight and then, with a scratching and a scrabbling, the rest of him disappeared from view and...wonder of wonders...the back gate swung silently open. Success! Tibbs must have landed on top of the handle and borne it down under his own weight.

George yapped in excitement and applause. *Well done, Mr Tibbs!*

George lost no time in entering his garden and saluting his friend. He congratulated himself that he had always kept the gate's lock and hinges well-oiled, otherwise this would never have worked. So now he was back on familiar soil and could take stock of the situation.

Mr Tibbs looked up at him. "What you gonna do, George? The wife's out canoodling with Smarmy Stephen so you can't get in to your house here. Wanna see what the two of them are up to over there?" Tibbs nodded in the direction of two gardens down.

Yes, George did. If they were up to no good then he was jolly well going to make them realise what he thought of it.

"C'mon, Tibbs, let's go a-visiting!" He leapt over the first fence and then the second until he was standing plumb in the middle of Smarmy Stephen's back garden. A couple of seconds later Mr Tibbs was with him, as curious as any cat would be, waiting to see what George was going to try.

The back dining room window was the first port of call. It was dark inside but there was no net curtain obstructing the view so George put his front paws up and craned his neck forward to get as close to the glass as he could. There was no movement he could detect in the interior.

"Can't see a thing here, Tibbs," George called down. "Are you sure they are both in?"

"Yeah...I think so. I suppose they could have gone out the front, but she don't usually do that... Here, let me have a look."

With that, Mr Tibbs ran up George's back and gingerly perched on his shoulder, peering into the window, his face close beside that of George's. Unorthodox, but neither of them could see a thing.

"Ow! Watch out!" George complained. "You've got sharp claws!"

Tibbs grinned: George could see his leering reflection in the window. "Never thought I'd ever do this to a dog!" Tibbs said. "Here we are, face to face, me sitting on your shoulder like a circus monkey!"

George dropped back down onto all fours. He shook Tibbs off at once.

"Brrr! Don't ever say that! I've had enough of circus jokes."

"Sorry. Touched a raw nerve?" Mr Tibbs picked himself up as if being tipped off window ledges was nothing unusual for him. It probably wasn't.

"Well they don't seem to be downstairs at least," said George. "I wonder if they *are* inside, but we just can't see them."

"Try to rouse them out of their hiding place, maybe? Kick up a racket?" Mr Tibbs was a practised renegade. He opened up his throat and let out an unearthly wail.

"Good idea, Tibbs. Let me try!"

George set off barking as loud as he could and then the two of them let rip together. It seemed like it was an awful noise from where they were standing in the enclosed space by Smarmy Stephen's back door but it still gained no reaction.

This was a direct challenge to the two animals' inventiveness. For Mr Tibbs in particular – who had had a cat's lifetime experience of annoying the neighbours in the dead of night – there was no holding back: he suddenly lit off around the garden howling like a demon and leaping on and over flowerpots, plants, watering cans, whatever he could find. It was truly inspirational and George just had to chase after him, barking maniacally and knocking into and over anything that was in his way. When the dustbin was bowled over with a tremendous *clang!* – spreading rubbish all over – that finally gained the desired result. A window opened above and a dishevelled head was thrust out, shouting angrily.

"Get out! Go away! What the hell...?" Smarmy Stephen was unexpectedly faced with a large greyhound that he'd never seen before in the process of wrecking his beloved garden. In amongst the utter chaos of a once-ordered environment he didn't notice Mr Tibbs, he saw only this half-crazed dog, bending down and getting hold of the spout of a watering can, growling and worrying it like a mad dog with a bone. It was enough to send him into apoplexy. Then a woman's voice shrilled out behind him.

"It's that black dog! The one which wrecked the college dining hall! Stevie! It's here!"

George looked up. He couldn't see her but it was his wife alright. His wife in Smarmy Stephen's bedroom! He erupted into a frenzy of barking.

"The dog's loopy! Completely nuts! And look what it's done to my garden – it's got to go!"

The head popped back into the bedroom and the window was shut. Smarmy Stephen was on his way downstairs and George readied himself outside the back door. It took a few moments before George could hear the clattering of feet. There was a momentary pause as the door was unlocked and then it flew open as the occupier charged out, brandishing a broom, expecting to confront the object of his fury somewhere down the garden. He did not expect a black greyhound flying past him, determined to gain entry to the house he was leaving.

George bundled his way past Smarmy Stephen, shot through the kitchen and bounded up the stairs. The internal layout of the rooms was exactly the same as his own house so he lost no time in reaching the bedroom and finding his wife. She to her horror was confronted with a large, angry dog that leapt onto the bed and, just a few feet from her face, gave vent to his feelings again in no uncertain manner.

Annabel shrunk back against the wall, her face draining of all colour. With Greyhound George facing her on the bed in the middle of the room she sidled around, anxious to reach the door and get away from this rabid nightmare. At the same time,

Smarmy Stephen was on his way back upstairs, drawn by the noise. George was never going to attack his wife but he was so upset at what he had found, seeing her only half–dressed, standing as he was on the rumpled bed sheets that must have been the scene of his spouse's infidelity, that he couldn't hold back from shouting at her and driving her from his sight. Annabel suddenly made a bolt for freedom just as her associate in debauchery came running into the room. Bang! They collided together and both fell over, rolling on the floor.

"Good grief!" hollered George. "Can't you two stop going at it, even for a second?"

Annabel scrambled on all fours out of the doorway, kneeing her partner in the groin as she clambered over him in her hurry to escape.

"Uuurgh!" Smarmy Stephen curled up in pain.

An appropriate goodbye present, thought George. Annabel had a habit of cleaning up and leaving no stone, so to speak, unturned wherever she visited.

But he wasn't done with her yet. George leapt over the grovelling carcass of Smarmy Stephen and, still barking crazily, chased his errant wife down the stairs, outside and through the rubbish-strewn garden and then through the back gate into the access road at the rear. Poor Annabel was clutching her clothes, and what decency she could muster, about her person as she scuttled along the back lane and from there, via the gate that Tibbs had opened, she fled into her own territory where she hoped to escape from persecution. But she wasn't quick enough. George was right behind all the way making horrible snarling noises, gnashing his teeth and trying to catch any trailing item of clothing. His anger had now subsided and what he really wanted was to get Annabel to run for shelter in her own home – thus allowing George to gain access himself. What Annabel would do when she realised she still couldn't shake off her pursuer he would have to wait and see.

Annabel scrabbled for her keys. Her denim jeans, pulled on in haste, were not completely zipped up and, frantic to get her hands into her pockets, she succeed in grasping her keys but only at the expense of pushing her trousers down just far enough to make her trip over. She found herself by her back door, rolling again on the ground with one hand trapped inside her jeans, the other trying to prop herself up and all the while a mad, noisy dog gambolling about all round her.

She whimpered in fear, frustration and desperation. It was such a plaintive and wretched sound that George almost felt sorry for her. Almost. He backed off to allow her to regain her feet but then he darted up and gave her a nip on the bottom.

"Go on, suffer, you unfaithful woman," he barked at her. "Don't think I'm leaving you and letting you get away with this yet!"

With a yelp, Annabel jumped forward, banging her head on the back door but finally withdrawing her keys. She fitted them in the lock, turned and opened up – then tried to get in and close the door behind her. George could see that coming and launched himself at his wife's rear end again, determined to jet-propel her into the kitchen and stop her from shutting him out. It worked. Annabel squeaked and flew into the house, holding on to an ample buttock to save if from further assault. She scampered straight through into the hallway and then, still screeching in alarm, she ran out of the front door, slamming it behind her. George caught sight of her terrified face rushing down the street outside; presumably back to the house and the arms of her chosen mate and partner in illicit enterprise.

George relaxed. His mission of gaining entry to his home had been accomplished, though it had to be said it wasn't in the way he had expected. He turned round and trotted out into the garden, being careful to ensure the back door remained open. He had a debt of gratitude to Mr Tibbs that he really had to pay off. He called out over the fences.

"Tibbs! You still there?"

"I should say so!" Tibbs jumped onto the fence to face his friend. "That just has to be the most entertaining episode to have occurred in this terrace in my entire life. And it's not just me who thinks so. Half the occupants of the houses around here have all been hanging out o' their windows enjoying the spectacle. George, old chap, why haven't you changed into dog more often before? This is tremendous! You're gonna be famous! Just wait 'til word gets around the low life that hangs out along these alleys and byways of the village. You'll have lines of admirers all waiting to see what you get up to next..."

George snorted. He thought Mr Tibbs was overdoing it a bit. "Come off it, Tibbs! You're a more disreputable character than me in these parts and with years more experience at it, too. I'm just bigger. And with a degenerate wife who needed some sorting out...not that she's seen the error of her ways, it seems. She back in there, d'you know?"

"Yeah. I heard their voices sounding off again just a moment ago." A thought struck Mr Tibbs. "Do you wanna come back and start all over? *Go on!*"

George gave a wry smile. "No – I've had enough of 'em. I'm back in my place now, so I've got what I want – but you start a caterwauling again if you want to. Let 'em know what us dumb animals think of their behaviour!"

George thanked his feline partner for all his support and went back indoors. His study was calling him. After an energetic day on the beach and now this climax of frenzied activity on his return home he decided it was time to rest. He could do with a shot of malt whisky to really finish him off but he sprawled out on the carpet below his desk without that pleasure and was anyway fast asleep within minutes.

In his slumbers, time passed and George became lost in dreams. Completely lost. He didn't know if he was an accountant at home, dreaming he was a dog; or a dog at home dreaming he was an accountant. In his troubled sleep he opened his eyes and thought he saw a trousered leg. Was he perhaps a man, dreaming he was a dog and that dog was dreaming he was a man? Certainly he felt as if he was a figment of someone else's dreams, if only he could find out who that someone was.

Now whether man or dog, in dreams or not, George had always liked puzzles – logical conundrums that needed a little concentration to figure them out. Suppose he was a greyhound, and had been all along, but had recently taken to dreaming he was a man. Then in his dreams the man-like world would seem very real...except on those occasions when the man of his dreams dreamt he was a dog. Would he then think the world was a very doggy sort of place but not believe it because he was dreaming? Somewhere in all of this, reality had gone missing.

George opened his eyes again, or dreamed he did. Looking about, he recognised his study which *seemed* reassuringly familiar – except that from his floor-level point of view it did have a sort of surreal quality about it. This was mildly disturbing. He closed his eyes.

Problems of logic did have an appeal to George's accountant mind. His job, or at least the one he dreamt he had, was all about sorting things out, putting the right figures in the right places and making sure they all added up as they should. But dreaming of the last few days and weeks he found himself being drawn to resort to ever-increasing anarchy – actually shaking things loose from their proper and comforting resting places and seeing what happened. It was an entirely creative process with absolutely unpredictable outcomes. One saw the world completely differently as a result, George realised. People, events, phenomena that previously acted and reacted in known and fairly well-worn trajectories now crashed about unhinged, releasing forces and bringing about consequences that were truly convention-shaking. It was inspiring!

Then George stood up. He stretched his arms and legs, shook his head a little and sat in his favourite study chair. His dogginess had worn off, or so it seemed. The house was quiet; it was early evening but still light in the long summer evenings. He wondered when Annabel would come home. He checked his pockets – there were his keys and his mobile phone, all of which had returned to him as he returned to human form. He really did wonder if he was dreaming: could such appearances and disappearances happen any other way? Atomic physics and research into parallel universes were not his particular forte so he couldn't answer that question. But he could phone Annabel – she had promised tea when he returned.

His wife did not have quite the sharp, businesslike, in-control voice she normally answered the phone with. In fact, she sounded just a little shaky.

"Annabel, dear, I'm home but you're not. Where are you?"

"Oh! Yes, George – I've just popped out. You did say you would phone before you got home, so why didn't you?"

Straight onto the attack, thought George.

"Sorry, forgot. Been out walking and the time just slipped away. Lovely afternoon. How about you?" George wondered what story she would cook up.

"It's been bedlam, since you ask. That wild dog that appeared in college has been running around everywhere here today and has wrecked Stevie's garden. I'm here now, er, helping to clean it up. Um...is everything OK with you at home..?"

This was a guarded question angling to know if a rabid, black greyhound was still in the house. George was momentarily tempted to say it was patrolling all around hoping to catch untrustworthy miscreants, but he didn't.

"Everything's fine, why shouldn't it be?"

"Nothing, no reason...did you want tea?"

"Mmm, don't worry. I'll get something myself... Probably go and buy a few things first...and for you too?"

"Um, no thanks, George. I've eaten during the day and don't want any more just yet. I'll be back in a little while when things are more ship-shape here."

Of course. George nodded, told his wife he'd sort himself out and would see her later. He rang off.

Speaking to his wife now, George felt numb. His anger at her infidelity had passed and what had replaced it was a sort of sad nothingness. He felt nothing for his wife. If he was honest, there had been nothing between them for some time but at least he had done nothing to undermine their marriage. He had not actively sought a liaison with anyone else. He had just rubbed along out of habit – comfortable, he supposed, in that work/home routine all chugged along nicely as always and no great changes were called for. He had put up with his wife's carping, complaining and criticisms – all her annoying idiosyncrasies – as he guessed she had put up with his. Of course he knew she enjoyed the company of a neighbour who shared her interest in horticulture and who was far more intent on putting on a show – a flashy, superficial face on things in order to impress society. George never had much time for such trivialities but Annabel was irresistibly attracted by it. Well, she had made her move now. There was no going back. George knew that he would have to confront her about it sometime and shake their relationship loose and let each of them go their own way. Apply the creative, anarchic option. It was just a pity that Annabel couldn't have been more honest and open about it before. He wondered how long her affair had been going on.

There was a slight problem, he realised, about how he was going to explain how he knew about her affair with Smarmy Stephen. Maybe leave it for the time being until evidence from a more reputable, more convincing source could be gathered? Trying to explain his greyhound transformations would only complicate matters exceedingly. He either would have to catch them in incriminating circumstances himself, in his human form

– not an altogether appealing thought – or maybe he could use the neighbours as the source of reliable information. According to Mr Tibbs, Annabel had been consorting with the enemy for some time so perhaps there were others, and not just four-footed ones, who had been witness to the adulterous couple's various comings and goings.

George needed a drink. Trying to think of ways to force the co-conspirators out into the open was straining his brain. He needed to relax his grey matter and release the creative juices, the neurons, the electro-magnetic discharges inside his skull. Let his subconscious mind take-off and find the solution. Single malt whisky was called for. Unfortunately the hip flask in George's desk was empty, so it meant going for fresh supplies. He knew precisely, of course, where his replacement bottle was hiding – it was probably still resting on the back seat of the red mini. A trip back into Durham was required.

Chapter 10

George went out for his Land Rover. He had decided to drive into Durham, recover his whisky and come back for a suitably fortified tea. It would not take him long and he reckoned he could be home again well before he saw Annabel return from Smarmy Stephen's. On his way to unlocking the garage he noticed Mr Tibbs hovering by the back gate. He stopped to fondle his head.

"Hi, Tibbs, remember me? Same person underneath – different species on the surface!" Since he could no longer address his friend in animal-speak he hoped his physical contact communicated the same message. Mr Tibbs looked at him and twitched his tail. George reckoned he'd got through.

Under George's hands the Land Rover roared into life and, carefully ensuring his feline compatriot was out of harm's way, George backed the motor out, span the wheel and set off out of the lane, out of the village, heading for the city, the red mini and the whisky that was waiting for him.

Carol and Sally were curled up on a sofa and an armchair, respectively, warming their hands on coffee and discussing the day's adventures when a ring on the doorbell disturbed them.

"Why, it's George! He's returned!" cried Carol, opening the door. "Back to join the human race and back to see us!"

"Thank you, Carol. Nice to be back, as you put it." He remained standing outside the door. "If you would be so kind, I've come to pick up my bottle of single malt...which I believe is still in your car?"

"No – it is inside now, and you must come inside as well if you wish to retrieve it." Carol stood aside and beckoned him in. "I think you know the way, don't you?"

George grimaced. Yes, he had seen all round this place earlier, though from an altogether lower horizon. Somehow, back in his human form, he was more nervous entering this female reserve and even Rosie – recognising his voice and coming out to see him – did not make him feel any more comfortable.

"George! Great to see you!" Sally welcomed him into the lounge. "And now as I remember you...before...before you animalised."

"Yes, yes, of course," George mumbled non-committedly, looking round for his bottle. He was anxious to remove himself as quickly as possible and not be drawn into prolonging his stay. Things had a habit of getting out of control with these two sirens.

Carol had other ideas. She had instantly read his mood and had no intention of letting him get away until he had delivered up some explanation for his amazing transformations. She stood in the lounge doorway behind him, blocking his retreat.

"The whisky is not in this room, George, and I'm not sure you should have it either, until you come clean first of all about what is it with your instant dogginess. How do you do it? And how do you turn back again?"

"*Do* sit down, George," prompted Sally, "and spill the beans! We are just itching to know. You are the first man-dog we've ever met. Are there others? And if so, where do you come from? I bet it's from a circu..."

"No!" George almost bit her head off with the strength of his retort. "Nothing to do with circuses or zoos or whatever crazy notions you come up with. I've told you before!"

"Go easy, George," smiled Carol soothingly. She didn't want to upset him. Clearly he was extremely sensitive about the topic and probably because he was still struggling to come to terms with it himself. "But I think you should give us some sort of explanation – if you can. Please?"

George refused to sit down. He walked over and put his back to the window, facing the two girls, his face lined with discontent. Rosie followed. He grumpily accepted that his hosts were bound to be fascinated by what had happened to him whilst he had been with them so he supposed he had better say something. Hopefully something brief enough to satisfy them and let him escape with his whisky without much loss of blood.

"OK...OK... But I can't tell you much." He looked around, somewhat like trapped animal, Carol thought, and dropped his hand to fondle Rosie.

"It has only happened after seeing you. Don't ask me why and don't get all psychoanalytical about it. But I think that Rosie has a key effect. Why a greyhound, for example? Maybe I've always wanted to be a dog?? I don't think so! All I know is that this never happened before I met you all. So I could say it's all your fault. Nothing more I can tell you, sorry!"

"What's it *feel* like, George, being a greyhound?" Carol was looking for a way to dig deeper, though she could see his resistance and the conflicting emotions in his face well enough.

George thought about that. He smiled slowly. "Fun!" he said.

"I should think so," said Sally, "looking at what you got up to on that golf course today. You enjoyed that, didn't you?"

George nodded. He didn't want to say how he felt at home, running after his unfaithful wife, however. He wanted his whisky and he wanted to get away. He didn't want to open up to all the feelings he had locked away inside. It showed. Carol knew. She went to fetch his bottle of Ardbeg.

George hurried to the front door and hovered there, waiting for his whisky. He turned to face Carol and say his goodbyes and thanks. He didn't want to look too closely at her young, appealing figure as she hurried towards him so he lowered his eyes as she reached forward. He didn't see the kiss coming, therefore, and he was for a moment completely immobilised.

He was shocked, embarrassed, flattered and he struggled to keep himself under control. He was clearly completely unused to anyone showing him any sort of love and affection. Something tugged at Carol's heart as she watched the complex of emotions flood over him. George managed to burble out his thanks and then he turned to go. Carol held his arm.

"I'm so pleased you came with us today, George, and so pleased you enjoyed yourself, too – I'd love to do something similar with you again...if you want to. Will you be too frightened to see us again – me, Sally and Rosie – if we *are* having that effect on you?"

George looked at her this time. She had lovely, searching green eyes that showed genuine concern. He could drown in those eyes.

"No...not frightened...yes, want to see you again." He was trying to hold everything in. "Got to go with this greyhound thing for as long as it happens. Got to sort it out, see. Can't run away from a thing like that. Anyway – must shoot for now. Thanks again."

Very quickly he gave Carol a return peck on the cheek. He waved to Rosie who was standing in the hallway behind her. Yep, he thought, it was definitely those two, most of all, who were turning his whole world upside down. As soon as he got back home he was going to open that bottle of Ardbeg. He walked quickly to the Land Rover and didn't dare to look back.

Carol watched him drive off, watched him deliberately ignoring her as she stood on the doorstep, trying to wave to him. Again, she knew.

George's emotions were in turmoil. He needed to get back to his village quickly but now, thinking of what had transpired just recently, even at home he would be unable to relax. He could not be happy at home any longer; those two sirens had made him increasingly unsatisfied at work, and facing Carol in particular – especially if she was kind and affectionate towards him – would make him liable to explode. George felt his world was beginning to fall apart; his head was throbbing just thinking about it as he drove along.

Thankfully it was a short drive and on this Saturday evening the traffic was light. George's concentration was all over the place but he managed to avoid any incident, parked his motor safely in the garage and, on an afterthought, did not lock the pull-down door. Similarly he opened his back gate and left it on the latch, unbolted, such that a push from outside would be sufficient to open it again. George looked round for Mr Tibbs as he walked up the garden path to his back door. He couldn't see him. That was a shame – he felt in need of a soul mate with whom he could commiserate.

Annabel had not returned from Smarmy Stephen's. George didn't know whether to be pleased or annoyed. Pleased he would be able to collapse in his study without her interference; annoyed that she was still out, presumably shamelessly cavorting with her neighbour again. This could not go on. George went into the kitchen, raided the fridge for something to eat, found a glass and then repaired to his study where he set up the bottle and glass on his desk before arranging his lanky frame in the chair.

The next half hour passed very pleasantly. He had cut himself a chunk of Cheddar from the fridge, placed that beside the glass and, exercising great self-control, took out his hip flask from the desk draw and filled it very carefully from the bottle of Ardbeg – not allowing a drop to stain the desk nor to enter his salivating throat. The flask was returned to the draw. He then splashed a fair slug of whisky into his glass, re-corked the bottle, took a bite of the cheese and slid back in his chair. Chewing slowly and deliberately, he raised his glass.

"Here's to dogginess!" he called out. He swallowed the Cheddar and sipped the single malt. Heaven! Relaxation spread through him from his centre outwards.

But thirty minutes of such recreation was all he was going to get. George had time to let his eyes wander around his study, looking at the various pictures he had put up – landscapes mostly; he had time to empty and refill his glass; he had time to cogitate a little on his singular transformations and what they all meant…and then the front door tentatively opened and Annabel came in, calling out for George as she did so.

"Coo-ee! I'm back. George! Where are you?" It was a nervous call, perhaps fearing a greyhound might emerge from somewhere.

George appeared in his study door, wondering how his wife was going to explain her long absence. Silly of him, he realised. Annabel went straight onto the offensive as soon as she saw him.

"George! Have you been drinking? I can smell the whisky from here! Is this your idea of making tea?"

"It was, in your absence," he replied sniffily. "What have you been up to all this time?"

"You know where I've been – helping to clean up at Stevie's after that crazy dog appeared there. It wrecked the garden and I don't put it past it to return and do more damage around here. You should've seen what it did at college – just the same. Damn filthy hound, it ought to be shot, and its owner too if ever it has one."

"Uh huh." George nodded. He wasn't going to get any sort of concession from her that maybe her place was in this house and not in someone else's. The suggestion that her place could be elsewhere, permanently, he might put to her later. He wasn't going to ignite that box of dynamite just yet. He shrugged his shoulders and returned to his study.

Annabel looked at her husband turn away and settle back in his chair with scarcely a comment. She was glad he had not questioned her more closely about where she had been and why it had allegedly taken so long to clean up a garden, but at the same time his seeming indifference to her activities and absence made her intensely annoyed. She thought of letting fly at him just to jerk him out of his closed little world but, considering she was relieved that her illicit liaison with Stephen Maxwell was as yet undiscovered she thought it was best to let sleeping dogs lie. She looked at him. What a dozy husband she had! Yes, that was a good analogy – he was about as energetic and as much fun as a sleeping, if not actually dead, dog.

That night, in their separate beds and unbeknownst to each other, Mr and Mrs Potts were having similar but opposing dreams. One dreamt of a romantic alliance being broken up by the appearance of a rabid and monstrous wolfhound; the other of luscious, untouchable women changing to a wild chase of an unfaithful partner from one house and garden to another.

Both visions were a rollicking, switch-back ride through hallucinatory experiences to finish eventually, for one dreamer, in the reassuring arms of a lothario and, for the other, in the reassuring arms of a familiar chair and a comfortable, single-malt-flavoured environment.

Annabel was the first to awake. It was Sunday morning but still she could not lie there contentedly with all sorts of disturbing images running though her mind. That bloody dog – first causing havoc in her nicely ordered college dining room; and then again with Stevie, in his bedroom no less, and chasing her through one house and another. She was glad it had disappeared but evil thoughts of it getting any closer to her were preventing any sleep.

Annabel Potts was a formidable advocate of order and discipline in this world. Unpredictable elements – especially dogs – were not welcome to it. One of her favourite sayings which she would regularly throw at her husband was: 'Everything in its place and a place for every thing.' George had begun to groan inside whenever he heard it – not so much for its repeated banality, not even because it seemed to delimit all of Annabel's tiny-minded world, but increasingly because that was what an accountant did at work – putting finances in order – and he was rapidly tiring of this and especially did not want to go home and meet the same desire to categorise, define, tie down and imprison everything there as well. Increasingly, at work and at home, *he* felt imprisoned.

But Annabel craved control in her life. If she could not for the time being control her dreams that Sunday morning, she would get up. The world had just better behave itself this day, that's all! She roused herself slowly from her bed, pulled back the curtains from the bedroom window and had every intention of starting the day with an altogether positive mindset, putting behind her any trace of nightmares...until she turned and saw what was sleeping in the place of her husband.

Animals did not belong in Annabel's universe. Any being that had a mind of its own and wanted to go places that Annabel did not approve of made her feel like screaming. Even garden worms that she dug up and which she found wriggled off in directions she did not permit, were fundamentally threatening to her view of an ordered and controlled environment. And dogs that did not stay in kennels, or on someone's tight lead, or locked away out of sight preferably in a steel cage on the Titanic – any such stray dogs should be shot.

Yet here, in her home, in her bedroom, in her husband's bed and slumbering under the bedclothes was a big, black greyhound. Her earlier injunction to let sleeping (or dead) dogs lie did not, she now realised, actually apply to any dog sleeping (or being dead) right next to her.

The lingering flavour of Islay whisky was the last thing of his dreams that George was able to enjoy – he was appreciatively savouring the last of it on his tongue and smacking his lips vigorously when he was suddenly aroused by a piercing shriek. It was a shriek to waken a stone statue; to shatter mirrors; to pierce the morning mist and frighten the birds in the distant woodlands. It was 6.00am in the morning, Annabel was standing on the other side of the room from George in her long nightdress and she was staring goggle-eyed at him and raising the roof with her screams.

"Oh bloody hell!" George groaned. He opened one eye to look at his wife. He knew in an instant what the problem was. He kicked all four legs to try and release himself from the bedclothes and as he did so the screeching went up a key and the decibel count climbed from deafening to seismic, wall-trembling intensity. Annabel had hearty lungs.

Greyhound George freed himself from all encumbrances, stood up on the bed and looked balefully at the woman in front of him. He tried to tell her to shut up. He was in a foul mood, being robbed of his sleep so early on a Sunday, but he conceded belatedly that perhaps his attitude was not one that Annabel would find too amenable. Certainly, angry dog language commanding the listener to pipe down a bit might be easily intelligible to other quadrupeds, even to two-footed and winged creatures, but hysterical middle-aged women of regimented routines and of blinkered perception did not fall into either category. Annabel's high-pitched and continuous shriek turned into a series of two-tone, but equally ear-splitting squawks – a bit like being shut in a room with a police or ambulance siren.

George gave up on her. He jumped off the bed and, glaring at the human occupant of the room, he turned towards the bedroom door. Annabel instantly dived to pick up a pillow off her bed and shake it at him. She was careful to keep hold of it, however, and keep it between her and dog.

"Go away! Shoo!" The squawking stopped and was replaced by insults. "You monster; you filthy, smelly, flea-bitten beast...I bet George smuggled you in here to give me a fright! He's done this, I just know it. I'll divorce him for sure now. Go on! Get OUT!"

Annabel shook the pillow again and was relieved to see the wild and hateful source of all her nightmares wander out of the bedroom and go trotting downstairs. She ran across and shut the door behind it. But now she was trapped and couldn't leave the room. This was intolerable! She would *murder* George for this. He must be the one responsible – there was no way else for that ugly, vicious creature to get into the house and into his bed. What a mean and spiteful mind he must have to go and find that beast and surreptitiously introduce it into the bed next to her whilst she was asleep! George had an evil mind and he had perpetrated a wicked deed. She would go to the lawyers now and insist on a divorce. She would claim psychological cruelty; that he was impossible to live with; that he was on the road to being criminally vindictive. And he smelled at night too – as much as that dog.

Annabel was thinking of all the ways she could use this frightening episode to build up a case in law against her husband. As she was doing so, she looked down out of the bedroom window to the back garden below and to her delight saw this fiendish black outlaw, this central evidence in her propaganda, saunter out amongst the rose bushes. Immediately she rushed to the bedroom door, flung it open, almost fell down the stairs in her haste and then flew to the back door where she locked it shut. Phew! She could relax now.

But what should she do? That nightmare of a hound should be done away with, permanently if possible, and quickly. It had caused enough problems in college and now it was here. It certainly should not be left to wander around and terrorise her home and others about – not Stevie's and not hers. She would be unable to rest. Would the council come and take it away? Possibly…but possibly not. Maybe she should find someone to take matters in hand immediately, with no fuss and bother, to finish with this dog and release her from the fear that this torment would suddenly reappear. Yes, that was the only sure solution. She would go and see Stevie. He'd do it.

George, meanwhile, had decided that, now he was up and in the best of canine health, he needed to take a run outside and exercise his finely tuned physique. He reckoned that like any high-tech, superbly balanced racing machine he needed to give it a blast to test all moving parts and blow away any dust and cobwebs that might be clogging his tubes. My! What enjoyment there was to be had in being a greyhound! He was raring to let loose. Mind, he was certain that as soon he was out of the house it would be locked and bolted behind him so he'd better take his keys with him. He didn't know when, or in what form, he would return. He fetched the keys from his study, levered down the back door and went into the garden. As before, he had left the back garden gate unbolted so it was just a matter of levering down the handle and going free. This achieved, he trotted over to the garage and, with a bit of effort, managed to raise the drop-down door sufficiently to get his head under and drop the keys behind the back wheel of the Land Rover. Job done. He was now ready for his run.

Bright and early Sunday morning the birds were still singing and George's heart was racing along with them. Oh to be free! He cantered over the first few yards of the footpath that led away from his village and zigzagged his way round the droppings of fat, overfed dogs that lazy owners had pushed into the field. Fifty or more yards of this and he thought he'd let rip. The hedgerow at the top of the rise beckoned and he wondered how quick he could make it.

The soft earth beneath his feet showered up behind him as he topped the rise in seconds. No contest! Where next? The hedgerow gave off a rainbow of different scents. His nose still needed training in this odoriferous dimension so he could only pick up a few. Rabbits? That was challenge. He immediately looked up and searched around. A sight hound, he looked immediately for any twitch of movement that would send him off like a homing missile. Nothing yet. But there was another smell or two he recognised: Rosie! Thinking on it, it wasn't so far from here where George first encountered her and her danger-ously attractive, unsettling owner. George's pulse was yet again pumping crazily at the thought of her. He reckoned the scent was old but nonetheless he shook his head and jumped skittishly away from this place where these two had obviously stopped a while ago.

George's own movement caused a clump of earth a short distance away to move as well. It wasn't a clump of earth – it was a rabbit! George was off in a flash. Whoopee! The joy of the chase! It wasn't so joyful for the poor bunny – a big, overconfident buck that had strayed a little too far from the hedgerow. The sight of open, slavering jaws and wicked-looking teeth coming in its direction at top speed made it dash for cover as fast as its legs could propel it. Not fast enough – George crashed into it like an express train and bowled it over a yard short of safety. Hooray! George was ecstatic – he'd won the race. Skidding to a halt and returning once more to his quarry he found the rabbit paralysed with fear. George stopped. This was no fun.

"Go on!" George said. "Run for it. I'm not gonna eat you!"

No reaction. The big buck was still frozen. In the distance however, there was more movement. The wind was in his face and George could pick up the scent of other dogs.

"Look," said George, "there's someone else coming now, so if you don't move quickly then some other hound will find you and you won't be so lucky. I was only playing but they won't be... Go on, shoot!"

Still no reaction. George lost interest in the petrified rabbit and looked at what appeared to be two Dalmatians coming in his direction. They had their heads down, sniffing the terrain and being upwind from George had not noticed him yet. Time for more fun. He'd charge into their midst and by the time introductions had been made all round the rabbit should have recovered from shock and found cover under the hedgerow. George didn't want to see murder committed on his account.

Off he charged once more, bouncing like a kangaroo as he closed on the other hounds.

"Hiya you two!" he barked cheerily. "What's doing?"

Nothing much, it turned out. It was a dog and a bitch who were friendly enough but there was something subdued about them. George was full of the joys of the early morning and leaping around as if on springs. The two Dalmatians were handsome-looking animals, they smiled at their new acquaintance, bouncing around and full of beans, but there was no boisterous doggy reaction as might have been expected. George's effervescence was not reciprocated.

"What's up?" George enquired.

Dog and bitch were slow to respond. They looked at George in envy; deferentially.

"You've not been *done*, have you..." said the dog. It wasn't a question, it was a statement. The bitch said nothing, only smiled again.

"Oh bloody hell!" said George. Of course they were handsome animals: that was what their owner wanted. Two Dalmatians that were good to look at; beautiful possessions; dogs as fashion accessories. They probably rode in a Range Rover. Here came the owner now, walking up with his stick at his side, dressed in his Barbour jacket, waxed cotton hat and Hunter wellies, calling his two pets. *Pets* for God's sake! George gave a howl and bounded off, glaring at the owner as he passed. He took a good look at him: tall, suntanned, glasses, striking-looking features – so that's what a dog castrator looked like!

"Bastard!" called out George. He raced off along the hedgerow.

It was two fields later that George slowed to a walk. He was still angry – with himself as much as anything. Domesticating animals, neutering them so that they fitted in to human-compatible environments, was the urban world he had come from. He had accepted that before but his perspective on that world had now, naturally enough, shifted considerably. He had a very personal appreciation of animal-kind at present and was glad he had never subscribed to the practice of emasculating dogs to make them more docile and acceptable. He shivered at the thought of it. He wondered also, in an idle, canine-wandering way as he happened upon a footpath that crossed in front of him, if there was anything that animals could do to get their own back.

Chapter 11

George took the path that crossed his present route because he knew it led eventually, after a somewhat circuitous journey, back to the minefield he had started in and from there, across the road to the access lane behind his own terrace. It was still early, and apart from one or two motors now parked in the lay-by on the road, he saw no signs of life. He trotted up the lane towards his garage and found to his surprise a welcoming committee.

"Here he comes!" called Mr Tibbs from atop the next-door garden shed.

"Hurrah!" barked a couple of dogs, waiting outside George's back garden gate. They were hairy mutts, one large with what looked like the strains of sheepdog hiding somewhere within the forest that sprouted all over him; the other was smaller, an indescribable mongrel with savaged ears and the look of having survived numerous fights. They both had bright eyes and the look of independent spirits about them. Neither had a collar. George warmed towards them at once.

"Hi guys," George offered in friendly mode, wagging his tail. "What's doing?"

"Just hanging around, waiting for you," said the savaged-eared mongrel. "We saw you go out earlier. Hadn't seen you before, but now we heard you're in the habit of chasing people round here."

"Yeah, Tibbs has told us all about it," said the sheepdog-like one. "Good for you. This woman makes a habit of throwing stones at us. So does the man further down. And we aren't doing any harm sniffing about these back alleys – why they gotta go and get all aggressive, eh?"

George commiserated. He thought he recognised them – a couple of strays that turned up now and again in the village, usually looking for titbits around the back of the local shop and the pub. He'd never paid much notice of them before, but now he enquired after their life stories. The bigger, hairier one was Rufus. An adorable puppy, he said, until he grew out of it and the family he was with tired of him. Drove him miles away from his home, which was somewhere in the south, took him for a walk in Durham woods and then disappeared, leaving him behind. "They left me worrying a bag of some meat or other and whilst I was busy trying to get into it, off they went. I heard the car drive away and thought they'd come back. No such luck!"

Then there was Mucker. He didn't have a real name – but he mucked about with anyone and everyone. Born in the back yard of some transport café on the motorway, a lorry driver had taken pity on him and carried him about for a bit, but then Mucker had got loose and the lorry drove off. "My fault," said Mucker. "Me being just too inquisitive, like. I got out and went sniffing round some petrol stop, and I guess my driver couldn't find me and had to go."

"Well, glad to make your acquaintance, the two of you," said George. "You came here looking for some action?"

Both dogs grinned. They yapped in agreement. They were definitely the fun-loving sort, always on the look-out for whatever opportunities life threw their way. These were not docile, domesticated, beaten-into-submission types. George wondered if there was a Range Rover they might visit locally.

"How about going to the footpath, nearby?" suggested George. "There're always people driving up on a Sunday to take their pets out for a walk there. Let's be sociable and go meet 'em." The possibilities of creative chaos were endless, he thought. "Wanna come, Tibbs?" George called up.

Mr Tibbs said he would follow at a distance. Gatherings of dogs were not his preferred company but he would find a tree, make himself comfy and watch whatever transpired.

The two cars in the lay-by had now spawned a third. The first there was not a Range Rover but a big Toyota, George saw. He wondered if the Dalmatians belonged to it, but until the occupants returned there was no way to know just yet. The footpath beckoned. The stile that led to it was the sort with a dog gate beside which Greyhound George had never bothered with – leaping athletically over the wooden barrier. Nonetheless it was very considerate of the council to provide local residents with this means to facilitate canine exercise; not that many dog owners strayed far from their cars.

George bounded over the stile in one. Mucker applauded vociferously but leant against the spring-loaded dog-gate. He was not the size to go leaping over metre-high obstacles and so chose the easier option. Rufus duly followed. Once inside the field the three dogs were of the same opinion – they shared the world with too many fat and unfit brothers and sisters that were a disgrace to the species. In fact there were a couple in front now – a golden Labrador and some sort of cross-bred spaniel. George went loping up to say hello.

Introductions were made without too much fuss. The owners of the two dogs were quickly ignored and within seconds all five dogs were racing around together, laughing, shouting and playing tag. George, naturally, was by far and away the most streamlined, supple and accomplished of all and drew admiring glances from the entire company. In particular, the golden Labrador, a bitch, was young and impressionable and took a real shine to this virile newcomer who apparently deferred to no human and exercised himself with no regard to the calling, whistling and other attempts to rein him under control.

The attractions of this circle of hounds all quite clearly enjoying their liberation then attracted the appearance of the two Dalmatians. Hooray! George was delighted to see them come running down from the hedgerow above and display a modicum of independence from their Barboured oppressor. He welcomed them with wholehearted enthusiasm. Five dogs had become seven and this called for some sort of celebration.

George quickly got the pack sorted. The first enterprise was a run across the field, east-west in V-formation, George taking the lead. That looked pretty neat, he thought: three dogs fanned out on his left, another three fanned out on the right. Then he thought they would look even better on the return run if the dogs were sorted in size: biggest in the centre, smallest on the wings. The west-east run drew gasps and applause from at least one of the attending owners. There was at least one discriminating human who could appreciate creative canine endeavour, it seemed.

What next? Mucker came running up, tongue hanging out and absolutely profuse in his felicitations. Being the wing-dog racing along at the perimeter he reported that he'd never before seen such an impressive display of poetry in motion. George thanked him but thought he was overdoing it a bit. Nonetheless, the standard had been set – how were they going to top that?

How about two oblique lines converging from either side of the field and running through each other? One dog from one side, alternating with one from the other like George had seen on motorbike displays? Neat idea but they were only seven hounds. It wouldn't work without a symmetrical number.

Then as if to answer his prayers, Rosie appeared. Rosie! She had galloped across as soon as she had seen what was going on in this field and George could not help but be delighted – symmetrical dog displays were now on the agenda. He gave an appreciative lick on Rosie's nose. He suggested – much to the chagrin of the golden Labrador – that Rosie take the lead in the opposite line to his own and quickly explained to all the idea of one dog passing between two of the opposite, in converging lines. There was a little doggy confusion about this at first but the Dalmatians knew exactly what he meant – one advantage of domestication was that they were accustomed to doing what they were told.

Off they went – four dogs in the southwest corner, four in the southeast. At the agreed bark they all set off running in single file converging on the middle of the field – largest first, smallest last. On passing through each other and arriving at the northeast and northwest corners of the field respectively then they did the return run – smallest first, largest last. Coming downhill this time they went faster and all had to be careful not to collide with their opposite numbers.

Success! A chorus of cheers and whistles went up this time – a number of walkers taking a Sunday stroll along the footpath had now joined the dog owners and the general opinion from all observers except the sour-faced man in the Barbour jacket was that this was first-class entertainment. The dogs themselves were all excited about their achievement. The Labrador bitch, mightily impressed by George's leadership, made it known that she was quite partial to the notion of producing puppies in great number with his assistance. In fact she would quite like to produce a veritable team of synchronised mongrel greyhounds if he might be persuaded to go home with her? George politely declined the offer, much as he was flattered and complimented by such female devotion, but he explained that he was a sworn celibate for reasons he couldn't go into just yet. No, he wasn't gay, he emphasised, but he possessed, er, a very volatile character and he could not approve of unstable fathers. Rosie, meanwhile, sidled up to the other bitch and whispered, quite emphatically in her ear, that she had better lay off for the moment or this older female would be forced to teach the younger an unforgettable lesson in pack hierarchy.

George noticed a nubile, tracksuited figure calling out from amongst the people assembled on the footpath. This required a decision. Had he finished with the formation running with his associates or not? He had the idea of maybe dancing, or even perhaps an imaginative design of dogs running backwards in unison? One thing he really fancied was them all sitting in a circle, raising their heads and howling out the same tune. The only doggy song he could think of at the moment was by The

Beatles: 'Hey Bulldog!' but he doubted he could teach others this if they didn't know it. OK, give it a rest for a bit.

So George called the pack together and suggested a few minutes' time-out. Rufus and Mucker said they'd thoroughly enjoyed themselves and they were up for anything else he wanted to try out, anytime; the two Dalmatians thanked George ruefully for showing them a more spirited side to life. Rosie came over, nuzzled his nose and suggested they go off and see Carol together. Meanwhile the Labrador bitch sat on her haunches and gave a little whimper. *Sod it all,* thought George, *you can't please everyone.*

Approaching the line of onlookers, George attracted a chorus of comments, nearly all appreciative. Rosie went straight up to Carol but George hovered back and made a show of accepting the plaudits. He nodded and smiled and bowed, much to the delight and amusement of his audience.

"You old rogue!" Carol caught his eye. "I never know when and in what guise I'll see you next…though I guess you enjoy giving everyone the run around…"

She grinned at the greyhound. He grinned back.

"Madam, do you know this animal?" asked a voice at Carol's side. It was the man in the Barbour jacket and Hunter boots.

"Sort of," Carol replied, still smiling. "I see him around now and again, but I'm getting to think my dog knows him better than I."

"Well, my dogs won't come back to me with him around. Where's his owner? He needs putting under control!"

"I don't think he has an owner," said Carol, looking back at Greyhound George. "He had one once but no one controls him now. I don't think he can even control himself these days. A right chameleon! Totally unpredictable."

George wuffed indignantly at this. Carol laughed but the Barbour man was not amused.

"I'll control him if he comes any closer, the brute!" He waved his stick at George and called him a few ripe names. He then shouted out again to summon his Dalmatians over. That annoyed George. He growled and bared his teeth. He was proud of his fine set of incisors (far better than the ivories he sported in his human form) and thought he'd give this unpleasant individual the full benefit of them. Grrrr! He snarled again, then he suddenly bounded away and went back to join the other dogs.

Hello! thought Carol. *What's he up to now?*

The Barbour man didn't think at all. He just kept shouting, waving his stick and cursing George from a distance. He then left the footpath and started off in the direction of the dogs in the attempt to get his pets to return to him.

Meanwhile George suggested one last manoeuvre to his pack of followers. He told the Dalmatians that he was sorry they had such tiresome owner but they were all going to put on a show that would shake him up a bit and enthral and delight everyone else. Were they ready?

Oh yes they were. So George laid out his plans, a particular choreography with a heroic role for Mucker, he said, that he was sure that Mucker would be pleased with.

And so the dance began. They started in single file but then on a signal bark each danced sideways, crossing one leg over the other, moving as a wave towards their audience. Another bark and the wave danced back, again crossing legs one over the other. Shouts, laughter and hoots of encouragement followed this display. It was the most comical performance possible – a line of prancing animals stepping it out together. The wave moved back and came close to the Barbour man – the only one of the audience that was not applauding this show. At last, George released the Dalmatians to approach their owner who stood still just in front of the crowd of onlookers with dogs converging upon him. George suddenly accelerated, leapt over the backs of the Dalmatians, up and in the face of their owner where he made as if to snap at him. Surprised, the poor man tried to step back only to find Mucker under his feet.

Over he went – plop! Down into the mud, rolling back with his feet in the air in this minefield of dogs' droppings. Another chorus of hoots and laughter went up. George ran a rapid circle around the man, barking and celebrating his downfall. More laughter from everyone except one furious and red-faced man covered in mud and dog manure. George bounced about one last time, calling out to all his fellow quadrupeds and saying cheerio – it was time to retreat and leave the assembled company to its own devices – dogs, owners, walkers and all. He raced away, back over the stile, across the road and off in the direction of his row of houses. He looked back as he did so – seeing Rufus and Mucker scampering after him, grinning like crazy, and beyond them, Carol in the distance waving goodbye and holding onto Rosie. The show was over.

As George cantered past the tree at the head of the access lane he noticed Mr Tibbs, high up in the branches.

"Get a good view?" he enquired.

"Yes thanks, George," the tabby cat replied. "Dog dancing – whatever next? Most enjoyable, but you'll never get me doing that!"

"Wouldn't try," barked George. He knew well enough that cats were solitary adventurers and any escapades with them would have to take that into account. His doggy buddies, however, were an altogether more sociable lot. George came to a halt outside his back garden gate and turned to meet his new pals.

"I think it's time to say goodbye for the time being," he said to Rufus and Mucker when they caught him up. "I'd rather like to take rest now… But how did you enjoy that?"

He needn't have asked. The two mongrels were tireless in their praise and appreciation of the morning's activities and George was forthwith invited to become a full member and honoured guest choreographer of the Durham Pack of strays, wastrels and reprobates. He was much affected by this generosity, thanked his friends profusely and promised to look in on their company whenever he was next in town and in the appropriate shape for adventure.

With snorts and snuffles all round, the three said their goodbyes. Actually quite tired now, George pattered over to his garage, wriggled his way under the door and searched for a spot to lie down. He never bothered to check his back garden gate – he was sure Bella would have locked it as soon as he had disappeared earlier so he found a place in the corner of the garage where he could pull down an old overcoat off a peg on the wall and spread it about just in front of the Land Rover. Neither in his human frame, nor as greyhound, was George endowed with rolls of fat, so a comfortable resting place was important to him. George kept a battered old clock on the workbench – he caught sight of it just before he flopped down. 7.30 am – it was still early. He fidgeted a bit to arrange the overcoat to his liking and then closed his eyes. He fell immediately asleep.

George woke up in pyjamas. That figured. He was wearing those when he doggified in the night so, as before, that was what he returned to when his alter-ego wore off. He got up from the overcoat and shook his aching frame. *I must remember to put something more comfortable down in the garage next time,* he told himself. *Better to be prepared for all eventualities.* He took a glance at his clock – goodness, only 7.40 am: he had been out only as long as it took to change shape, it seemed.

His metamorphoses intrigued him now. He didn't *feel* anything. Switching from one to another always seemed to happen when he was asleep so there was no sense of travelling into another reality with flashing lights and electronic sounds like he had seen in numerous science-fiction films and television programmes. He wondered if it was all a state of mind that brought it on and brought it off. He had an inkling of what caused it, he reckoned it was a need to escape – he feared to dwell upon that now – and then when he had been a greyhound for a while it seemed his mind had relaxed enough for him to return to human form again.

So be it – time to follow a human lifestyle now. George recovered his keys from under the Land Rover and lifted and lowered the drop-down door sufficiently to let himself out. He didn't close it completely behind him but left a little gap, sufficient for a dog to insert a head and heave it up a fraction. Again he was pleased with himself for keeping the door mechanism well-oiled and easy enough for someone half his size to manipulate. Then he crossed over to his back gate, fully expecting it be bolted on the inside so that he would have to walk round to the front of the row of houses and let himself in by his front door. But no – not only was it not bolted, but it was not even closed to. The gate yielded to the slightest push – indeed it was as he had left it when he exited on four legs earlier…though he could have sworn it was not like that on his return: hence his recourse to the garage. George stood for a second, wondering if he had been mistaken.

He opened the gate a little more and stepped inside – only to find Smarmy Stephen hiding within, his expression fixed hard and holding a cricket bat above his head.

"Looking for a game, Stephen?" asked George pleasantly. "Didn't know you were a sportsman."

"Um…no."

"Bit cramped in here, don't you think?" George continued. "You'd be better off going down to the recreation grounds."

"Yes…no…" Smarmy Stephen was a little at a loss, not expecting the master of the property to be returning at that moment. "I wasn't thinking of playing cricket."

"Just thought you'd lay me out in my own garden then?" asked George. "Your idea of neighbourly fun and games, is it?"

"No, no, I was waiting for a dog…"

"Of course. In my own garden. Playing bat and ball with a dog. In amongst the rose bushes. You feeling all right today, Stephen?"

Before he could answer, Annabel looked out of the kitchen door. Hearing voices, she wanted to know what was happening. Naturally enough, seeing her husband, she resorted to frontal assault.

"George! What*ever* are you doing here in your pyjamas?"

"Hello, Annabel. I live here, didn't you know? Went out for a breather. Took the morning air. Went to freshen myself up, that sort of thing."

"Don't be so sarcastic, George. It doesn't suit you. And don't try and deny you put that evil dog in the bedroom with me. Wicked! Spiteful! Unspeakably malicious of you! I know what you're up to – you're trying to make the worst of my nightmares come true."

"Put a dog into bed with you? Nothing of the sort, my dear. I went out. True. In my pyjamas, true. But what is in your nightmares is down to your own guilty and clearly very fertile conscience and I have no responsibility for what you dream up. Now, what Stephen Maxwell is doing in our garden with a cricket bat I would have thought you might have questioned? *He* doesn't live here...at least not to my knowledge, though goodness knows what goes on here when my back is turned."

Annabel's face blushed to the roots of her hair but she wasn't conceding anything. "There's nothing going on here other than trying to catch a big, black, vicious dog. I saw it outside only ten or fifteen minutes ago. You weren't here, so I asked Stevie..."

George looked around the garden. He made a point of poking his head outside the back gate and looking up and down the lane outside.

"There are no black dogs anywhere in sight. In fact I've never seen any vicious black dogs within *miles* of this place...unless you are talking about that fat, waddling Labrador who lives across the lane from here and is about as menacing as the cold rice pudding his owner feeds him on occasions." George turned to address Stephen Maxwell. "Stephen, I think you and your cricket bat should go home now. Nice to know you once played the summer game, very civilised of you, but leave my wife and her hallucinations to me now, thank you." There was a note of finality in his voice.

To his credit, Stephen Maxwell snorted and did as he was bid. George could see he was somewhat fed up standing sentry duty for a non-existent dog.

Annabel was beside herself, however. "I was not hallucinating! There *was* a dog outside just a few moments ago. The one that was in the bedroom with me – in *your* bed – the same one that has been terrorising the neighbourhood around here. And you are the only one who could have put it there!"

"Yes, dear, of course. I went out and fetched it in the middle of the night, did I? Put it to bed next to you without either of us making a sound? Of course I did. But look! It's gone now so there's no need to worry. Let's have breakfast…"

Annabel fumed and protested but George wasn't listening. In fact, he felt rather pleased with himself. It had been no part of his intention that night to wake up and terrify his wife, but the way things had turned out he had in some measure got back at Annabel for her infidelity. And he'd now managed to make Stephen Maxwell look a bit of a simpleton too. That and the morning's display of canine creativity that had ridiculed the dog castrator, all in all, it had been a good hour or so's work. George whistled contentedly, if not exactly tunefully, as he fried egg and bacon and served the same to his wife and himself. Annabel sat and consumed it all with hardly a word; her face was a picture of frustration and fury and George could see she dearly wished to pin all the accusations on her husband and if possible nail him to the floor with them…but it wasn't going to work. Annabel would have to admit that her story would stretch the credulity of even the most wife-friendly of divorce lawyers.

The Sunday papers had been delivered so, after breakfast, still in his pyjamas but now covered with a dressing gown, George retired to his study and devoted a couple of hours to reading them through. He didn't usually spend so much time perusing the press but after his run out, and the excitement that had both preceded and terminated that exercise, he didn't feel like doing anything much just yet. And single malt whisky went down well with the sports section – especially since Newcastle United had just won at home. George was smilingly content with life.

Annabel meanwhile was not at all happy. She was convinced that George had something to do with the appearance and disappearance of the Hound of Saint Bartholomew's this morning but there was no way she could prove it. She went out to prune the roses, not that they really needed it but Annabel needed to. She went up and down examining each bush. She looked at every leaf, every bud, every stalk and detail on the standard roses. She muttered under her breath; she muttered out loud; she even found herself issuing a number of quite inventive curses. After several rounds of clippings and curses, she went and fetched the garden rake – a good excuse to clear the lawn of the debris from the roses and also to aerate it. A few savage strokes with the rake turned out to be remarkably good therapy – especially thinking of how someone's head could also be quite effectively aerated like this. Brandishing the rake quite flagrantly in one hand and thinking such heart-warming thoughts, she talked to the roses quite animatedly – asking them what should she do and how could she somehow rid herself of dog, nightmares and husband? They were all interlinked, she was absolutely certain. Maybe, just maybe...the thought came to her in a flash...maybe George and that damn dog were one and the same? She stopped and thought about that: a ridiculous idea, but nonetheless there was an infuriating similarity in their characters. If she could get rid of one of them, perhaps the other would disappear as well? That would certainly be the test of her supposition. And what a liberation it would be for her as well. Annabel Potts resumed raking with renewed savagery.

Chapter 12

Recently-retired Professor Geoffrey Collins O.B.E. was approaching his 67th birthday. As the ex-Master of St Bartholomew's College, University of Durham, he had been invited to a Formal Dinner back at his old haunts to celebrate his anniversary. He telephoned the current Master of College, Dr Jonathan Adams, to confirm.

"Who's going to be there for this dinner, Jonathan?" Professor Collins asked.

"Up to you, old fruit," replied Dr Adams. "It's your do; who do you want to invite?"

"Um, well it had better be open to the members of the Senior Common Room, as normal, but you know what, you've appointed a number of new staff this year, haven't you? I'd rather like to meet them and see how they're getting on. Gotta keep in touch, don't y'know."

"Of course. And you've heard about two of them I'm sure... Still got an eye for the ladies, eh, Geoffrey?"

Professor Geoffrey Collins harrumphed. His successor had hit it in one. "I don't know what you're talking about," he laughed.

"No, I'm sure you don't," laughed Dr Adams in return. "But don't worry, I'll make sure that our new Student Welfare Officer and her friend from Psychology both come along. I'll send them personal invitations, though you won't be the only one wanting to talk to them. They've certainly shaken up the Senior Common Room and in addition half the young men in the JCR seem to want welfare appointments. I never knew we had so many problem students!"

"So I've heard, Jon. So I've heard. But good that you've got some young blood in. Too many of us old fogies dominate the place. What's the dress code for the evening?"

"We were thinking of a black tie dinner: DJs for men; long

dresses for women. Four course meal; candles; silverware, the works. SCR funds will stretch to some decent plonk for High Table, too. We'd like to put on a bit of a show for you and as it's the last Formal of the academic year you know that the students like to go out in style as well. What do you think?"

"Sounds good to me. I'll know most of the graduating class so will be glad of an opportunity to say goodbye to them. And both old friends and new in the SCR should together make it a most enjoyable evening. Many, many thanks for the invitation. Very kind of you." Prof Collins was smiling with anticipation as he put the phone down.

Formal Dinners at St Bart's were a popular and well-established tradition. They were an excuse for members of the college – from first-year students to long-serving academic tutors – to dress smartly, put on academic gowns and take a waitress-served meal all together. Not that the staff and students mixed very much. There were a restricted number of places for academic staff and guests – members of the Senior Common Room – on High Table and the students of the Junior Common Room were allocated places apart on Low Tables around the rest of the dining hall. There was an extra fee charged for such Formal meals, distinct from the usual buffet service at college, and the fee was even higher for the grander occasions, as was being proposed for the ex-Master's birthday celebration. Despite the cost, however, the popularity of especially this last Formal of the academic year meant that the dining hall would be packed.

Carol Davies, Student Welfare Officer at St Bart's, found a nicely embossed invitation to the final Formal Dinner of the academic calendar waiting for her on her desk when she arrived for work, 9.00am Monday morning. It was to be on Friday week: in twelve days' time. She immediately phoned Julie, the College Secretary.

"What's all this, Julie?" she enquired. "I've never received an invitation to a Formal meal like this before."

"I know," replied Julie, "but on this occasion the Master wanted you and Sally in particular to come. Since it is the last Formal, there'll be a rush to reserve places on High Table so I got the message to send you invites first of all."

"Any reason why we're so honoured?"

"Yes. It's a special request from Professor Collins on this occasion of his birthday. He was Master here a couple of years back – before Dr Adams and before you were appointed. He's a real dear, you must have heard of him. Apparently he wants to meet the new staff and new members of the SCR. And I think he knows you've made a bit of a splash since you've been here so I guess he wants to see what all the fuss is about."

"Have I been causing a fuss?"

"Come on, Carol! You know you have. So of course Professor Collins wants to meet you. But don't worry – like I say, he's a real dear. Most of us love him and I'm sure he'll be quite taken by you. And Sally. You've both been sent invites."

"Can we bring partners?"

"Usually that's OK. Both the Master and the ex-Master will be bringing their wives so you are entitled to do so if you wish. But you had better confirm places before all seats are taken."

"Right. Then can you confirm for us both? I know Sally will want to come and we will both be bringing partners. Reserve us four seats can you?"

"Will do. You sure you want four?"

"Absolutely!"

"OK. It's done. Some of our boys will be quite disappointed you're bringing a partner, but you know what they're like!"

"I do. And they're just boys, so there's no contest. Thanks, Julie, you're an angel." Carol rang off.

That evening, Carol and Sally discussed their invitations. They didn't normally go to Formal meals at the college but on this occasion, given the personal nature of the Master's and the ex-Master's summons it would have been rude as well as unpolitic to decline the offer.

"Trouble is, many of the stuffed shirts of the SCR are just not my sort of company," complained Sally.

"I know. That's why I reserved places for partners; I thought you'd like that. Are you going to ask Duncan to accompany you?" Duncan was a friend from their undergraduate days who had been chasing Sally for years.

Sally smiled. "Of course. I've gotta give him something now and again to keep him hanging on!"

"You're awful, Sal. When are you going to settle down with him?"

"Dunno. Not yet, that's all. He'll be great for the SCR – they won't know what hits them when he's had a few – but can I live with him? Not yet! What about you – who are you going to take?"

"I've not stopped thinking about that all day. You know who I want, don't you?"

"Yes...but would he come?"

"If I insist, I think he will. But am I being selfish? Is such a Formal, with all the SCR there, going to be his thing?"

"Probably not, no more than it is for us. But I'd like to see him there and see how he interacts with them...and it will be fun to see how he and Duncan get on."

"Yes..." Carol was very introspective. "The thing is...I want to get to know him better and it's so difficult when I don't know how long I'll have him before he changes out of his skin again..."

"Well, we've talked about this for *ever*. You're part of the reason; the biggest part, in my view, for his shyness and inability to share our company. We both know it and he knows it too, so we're doing him a favour in forcing him to confront you and his own feelings for you." Sally grinned. "The Formal Dinner will be the crucial test to see how long he survives. It is going to be fascinating – you've *got* to invite him. Do it now. I'll call Duncan as well..."

It was decided.

* * *

Late Monday evening and Annabel's mobile buzzed. It was Stephen Maxwell. Annabel made sure her husband was ensconced in his study with the door shut before she answered.

"Hello, Stevie, my love. How are you?"

"Fine, fine, Annabel. I've got some good news for you."

"Oh yes? Do tell."

"Well I've been doing some digging. You know you mentioned you wanted that greyhound got rid of as soon as possible, yes? Well there are people in the dog racing business that can help."

"Oh, Stevie, you are a wonder. What have you found out?"

"It's all very hush hush, so don't breathe a word of this...but every year there are tens of thousands of greyhounds that are retired from racing and have to be disposed of. Illegal to kill them, o' course, but who's gonna take all them dogs, eh? There's a racing kennel near us that pays people to take 'em away, no questions asked. Well – I followed up a lead there and found someone who can help."

"I don't want that mutt just taken away, Stevie. I want it dead – stone-cold dead. It can't ever invade my nightmares – not ever again!"

"Yes, yes, Annabel, I know. This man'll do it. He lives on a farm up Weardale somewhere, so I understand. Met him in a pub this afternoon and we had a long talk. But like I say, you gotta keep this quiet. He's got a captive bolt gun from an abattoir; he's done for any number of dogs already and buried 'em up on the moors, above the farm. It'll cost a bit but he'll do it if we can catch that animal."

"We gotta catch it first? If we do, will he come straight away? I don't want that damned dog causing any trouble and letting everyone know we've got him. You know the noise it makes!"

"Yeah, I thought of that. He says it'll take him a couple of hours to get to Durham…but it will be quicker if we can advise him beforehand so he's standing by. He doesn't want anyone knowing about his business either so the quicker the better for him as well. Says he's got a Transit van and he can do the business there and then as soon as he gets the dog inside. Shooting the gun off makes a noise, he says, but it's no different from someone banging the van door loudly. There's no blood, no mess, no incriminating evidence afterwards. 'Cept a dead dog, of course, but he'll dispose of that."

"Oooh, Stevie! This sounds just what we're looking for, you lovely man. Well – that's settled it, then. We gotta catch the beast next time we see him around here. That may not be so easy…"

"It'll be easier, my love, if you don't run off screaming when you see it. Just give me a call and I'll come round quick as I can. Of course, it will be better if we can trap it in the house or somewhere first of all. And George mustn't know or he'll let the dog out of the bag, so to speak."

"Yes. It will have to be when he's at work, or out or something. So far, I've only ever seen that mutt when he isn't around which seems pretty incriminating. I reckon he finds that dog somewhere and releases it near me – either in college or at home – just to get at me. So if we can turn the tables on his plans that will suit me just fine. Thanks for the call, Stevie. You've made it so that I'm almost looking forward to seeing that brute of a dog this time. Brilliant! I love you!"

The rest of the call between the two of them descended into a series of snuffles and woffles and baby talk but the conclusion to their conversation was not infantile at all. It was murderously serious.

* * *

Late Monday evening and George's mobile buzzed. It was Carol Davies. George looked round and made sure his study door was shut before he answered.

"George, you're coming out with me on Friday evening next week.. Book it in your diary right now because I'm not taking no for an answer."

"Is that so?" George replied. "I'm going out with you, am I? And just what sort of evening have you got planned for us?"

"It is going to be a very elegant Formal meal and I need someone like you to come with me and chaperone and protect me."

George laughed. That was a good one. "Who's going to protect me from you then? And is Sally going? Will I need protection from her as well?"

"Now, George, you're being obstructive – and ridiculous. You don't need any protection from either of us, only from yourself if you get some wild notion to change shape again. Besides, Duncan's coming. You'll like him."

"Who's Duncan?"

"Duncan Mackay. A friend of Sally's. Her *special* friend...and he's almost as wayward and unpredictable as you."

"I'm unpredictable? What about the two of you? I never know what you're going to throw at me next. Just exactly what is this elegant meal you are trying to drag me into?"

"It's a college Formal. Sally and I have received special invitations and we're only going if you and Duncan go with us."

"Right. So you're not going then."

"Now don't be awkward. Of course we are going. And I need you to go with me as my chaperone, I've told you that." Carol knew perfectly well that George would normally want to run a mile in the opposite direction from university functions, but by playing up her need for 'protection', she reckoned George would be too much of a gentleman to turn her down. Nonetheless, the required protestations would have to be gone through first.

"Carol, you cannot take me to one of those awful academic get-togethers. They'll either be talking a lot of wishy-washy codswallop that will be of no interest to me, or they'll be swanking around with their noses in the air and pretending they are all terribly important. Absolutely not. Not my scene at all. No way. You cannot do this to me."

"George, it's you that's talking a lot of wishy-washy codswallop. You haven't a clue what some of these people are like. Some of them are really nice, friendly and courteous; feet solidly on the ground; quite, quite normal…certainly not liable to turn into monsters, gargoyles or greyhounds at a moment's notice. And I want you with me to fend off any dogs who want to get too friendly. You're not going to be one of those dogs, are you? Tell me you're not…"

That was a low blow. A sensitive individual, George's feelings were hurt. He half suspected that he turned into a greyhound (goodness knows how) as his last defence against this staggeringly beautiful female that he found simply oozing with sex, sensuality and desirability. She was irresistible. In fact the only way he could resist her was to swallow bucket-loads of alcohol and pass out. He went silent.

"George?" Carol instantly regretted what she had said. She could feel his hurt down the other end of the phone.

"I won't get too friendly," George replied, his voice flat and quiet. "Easy for you – I won't go. Neither as man nor dog."

"George, I'm sorry." Carol was alarmed. "I didn't mean it to sound like that. I really didn't. I love you to bits, George, and you are the only one that I want to get friendly with…and as a man, not as a dog. No one else. Understand, George? Are you listening? Talk to me. I really, *really* want you to go with me. Please! I can't go alone…"

George was struggling with his feelings. "I'm still here. I'm thinking. Let me call you back." He put the phone down.

"*SHIT!*" As the line went dead, Carol swore loudly and threw her mobile down. Sally looked at her in concern.

"Shit, shit, shit! I really screwed that up!" Carol was mad with herself. "Now he won't want to see me again. Oh, Sally, how could I be so stupid and say everything wrong like that? What is it with me and men? I'm sick to death of all these arrogant machos and narcissists and then I find this shy, gentle, absolutely adorable one who is totally bewitching and I come over like an arrogant, pushy feminist and insult him right down to his marrow. But dog or man, I *love* him!"

This confession, out loud to herself and to her best friend, brought tears to her eyes. How was she ever going to rescue the situation?

Meanwhile, not so very far away in the nearby village, George was still struggling. He turned to his desk draw and pulled out the whisky flask. He looked at it. Then he put it back, unopened. No – not this time – he was going to think it through and not retreat into an alcoholic haze.

What was he going to do with his life? He was married, he admitted to himself, very unhappily now and had kept it together out of force of habit, no more. His wife had been bolder than he and had done something about it – throwing herself into the arms of a neighbour. Could he really object to that? He had not wanted to confront the awful truth that he had wasted years of his life with her and he guessed she had not wanted to question things too deeply either. And now there was this glorious twenty-something young siren that had somehow swam into his life and he was almost too frightened to look at her. Moreover, she had just told him she loved him to bits. What was he going to do about that? Run away from her?

The fact was that George didn't really believe her. He was an unattractive, hopeless old fool and he knew that if he got emotionally involved with her he'd only get hurt when some more attractive, intelligent and sophisticated young man came into her orbit. And he'd be left looking like a stupid old geezer that should have known better than to act like a gormless, love-struck teenager. He had better not see her again. He really ought to get himself under control.

But then again, why couldn't he get his feelings under control? OK, she might be the sexiest thing he had ever seen – either on two or four legs – why not just admit that to himself and go along with it for wherever it took him? If she eventually tired of him and found another, well – what had he lost? It would be a roller-coaster of a ride while it lasted. And he simply had to get his feelings under tighter control. What was he? Man or mouse? Or greyhound? He was not some fragile, emotional teenager any longer. Call her back and say he wanted to go out with her – damn it all – wherever it led in the future. He picked up the phone.

When Carol's mobile sounded she dived upon it like a shark taking a victim. It was George calling! She could barely speak.

"George! I'm…I'm sorry…what can I…"

"Listen woman…" George's spirits were rising. He had made his decision. He was not going to let this or any other female play with his feelings any more. He was going to lay it on the line. "…I'll go with you, OK? I'll go to this bloody Formal Dinner and you had better introduce me to some normal, decent people and not some fancy, pretentious, high-falutin professors or whatever who are too snotty and superior. And tell me more about this Duncan. How do you know if I'll like him? Where's he from?"

Carol was holding back the floodgates in relief. "Inverness. Oh, George – *thank you!* Of course you'll like him: he's a mad Scotsman we knew at Edinburgh Uni. Half wild, so Sally was enamoured with him right from the outset."

"Is he another academic?" George asked suspiciously.

"Not sure what you mean by that. He doesn't work at university, if that's what you mean, no. He's got a proper job. But *I* work at university. *I'm* an academic, if you like. Is that so bad?"

"Hmmph!" George hmmphed. "In your case, no. Well, I'm not so sure now I think about it. Dunno if I know you well enough yet."

Carol's heart soared. Not *yet*! That meant he wanted to know her better. "Well, if you come with me next Friday and promise not to change into a greyhound all night you can get to know me *loads* better. In fact, George, it doesn't just have to be next Friday, you know… A girl might like to receive offers at times and not have to make all the running herself…"

George hmmphed again. Yes. He supposed she might. He'd got himself into this…he had better get himself out. "Alright. Alright. We'll see how it goes. If you behave yourself at this dinner of yours, then next time I'll call you. OK? Right! Bye for now." He put the phone down hurriedly. He'd committed himself now.

Not so far away in nearby Durham, Carol whooped. She put her phone down more carefully this time and did a little dance in front of her soul mate.

"Whoopee! Got him! Hooked! He's come back to me! He even said that if all goes well, he'd ask me out next time. Oh, Christ, Sally – am I going crazy? One extreme to another!"

Sally sniffed. "Yeah, I think so. You're getting to be a sad case, falling for a dog-man."

"Do you think I can confront him about that, Sal? Get him to confess his feelings? Do you think I should? Or is it too soon for him? You know what men are like – they're never in touch with their emotions."

"Dunno, Carol. You know him better than I. You could try, I guess. Why not ask him how he does it, change shape and all, and suggest that he help you do the same too – become a bitch when he becomes a dog? That would be fun!"

Carol whooped in laughter. "I've had men call me a bitch before but that never achieved anything. But this time, I'd simply love it if he called me that! What sexual possibilities that offers up!" She hooted in laughter again. "Dunno if I should think about that…"

Both girls laughed together. The evening had finally turned

out well: Sally had already contacted Duncan so the foursome looked confirmed. The Formal Dinner next week couldn't come fast enough.

George thought about it all night in his single bed, across the room from the wife he'd lost contact with, lost feelings for, years ago. He had been invited to attend the next Formal Dinner at St Bart's. He supposed this was in fact quite an honour – he'd heard about them for years from Bella who, in private, had always turned her nose up at such ceremonial functions, though she could hardly make that view known since it was her job to help prepare and then tidy up after them.

But it wasn't the dressy procedures; the important guests, nor even the eclectic small talk that such an occasion was bound to feature that worried him, it was just wondering where this was all leading and, indeed, what he himself wanted out of the evening. He didn't know university folk at all. Carol was right on that score: he didn't have a clue what they were really like. He had only his own prejudices, formed of course in a life that had been excluded from their circle. Thinking on it, he ruefully admitted that academics were probably no different than any other collective group of professionals and he mustn't let other people's prejudices, especially those of his wife, influence him.

And as for where this was all leading? Well, he had decided to throw all caution to the wind and just go for it. Stop being such a nervous, frightened old fart and start acting like the circus entertainer or lion tamer or whatever it was those girls mistook him for. Yep – that was the strategy. No turning back. With that, George turned over and went to sleep.

Chapter 13

Annabel was surprised – no, amazed – that George had been invited to a Formal Dinner at St Bart's. She was instantly jealous, never mind that such pompous events she had always poured scorn upon in the past. What had George, of all people, done to deserve such an honour?

"I'm not sure," said George, honestly enough, when Annabel demanded an explanation. "I met this girl from St Bart's out walking with a dog. Nice dog – a greyhound which seemed to like me..."

"A *greyhound*! Not that awful black villain that has been causing so much trouble?"

"No. Not at all. Sandy-coloured bitch. Well-behaved and really friendly. We got on exceedingly well." George smiled at his wife's discomfort at the mere thought of his canine alter-ego.

Annabel knew about that dog – it belonged to the new, young Student Welfare Officer who had been causing such a stir in college. She couldn't stand the sight of her – too pushy, too full of herself by far. She broke the rules in the first week with having that dog in college and she had been breaking them ever since, though nobody did anything about it. Everyone taken in by her pretty face and nice smile, of course. So what was she playing at, inviting George to the Formal? And what was George thinking of? What a short-sighted buffoon he was! Couldn't he see he was just being suckered into an occasion where she was going to make a fool out of him? Well, he had it coming, Annabel thought bad-temperedly.

George quite enjoyed his wife's irritableness. After all this time disparaging these ceremonial functions that she claimed were just for laughable, overdressed posers, she was actually quite vexed that her husband and not herself would being going to one. Her mood did not improve when George came back from town the next Thursday having hired the dinner jacket, dress shirt, black tie – the works. He actually had his own full dress uniform somewhere packed away which he hadn't worn for years but it signalled the importance he gave to this dinner invitation that he wanted to look his best and was not going to dig out his old, dusty, moth-eaten alternative.

Friday evening came and Annabel's mood soured even more as George came downstairs in his new get-up and waited in his study, pottering about for the car that was going to pick him up. The fact that she would use her husband's absence to go shooting down the lane and disappear into another's house and his enthusiastic embrace was not, for the first time, enough to lighten up her long face. George had guessed what she would be doing, of course, and well, he thought, she was stuck with the consequences; she'd chosen the sort of company she preferred. She was welcome to him. Meanwhile he was feeling really rather chipper: his mobile had just warned him that the car was on its way.

There was a *toot-toot* that broke the stilted atmosphere in the house and George hopped smartly out front to find a long, grey Volvo waiting for him. A rear door opened to welcome him in.

"Hello, girls, new chariot?" George said as he clambered aboard.

"Hello, George," replied Carol from the front seat. "Say hello to Duncan beside you. It's his car, but we're not letting him drive."

A ginger-haired man with freckles grinned at him from the rear seat and offered a hand. George shook it as he settled himself behind Carol in the front passenger seat.

"Hello, Duncan. I see these girls have got you sorted already. You known them long?"

"Aye, since university." He spoke with a soft Scottish accent.

"We met at Edinburgh," called out Sally as she drove off.

"He's a mad Scotsman who always gets drunk and starts a fight," said Carol, "so we're driving tonight."

"So, Duncan, if you've known them for some time, poor man, are you're still sane?" asked George.

"Och...I dunno 'bout that," replied Duncan "What's sanity, after all? Impossible to measure. How long have you known these two?"

"Duncan's a G.P. He's got a practice in Newcastle," Sally shouted back as she negotiated a turn out of the village and onto the main Durham road.

George nodded, thinking about his own mental state. "I met these girls some four or five weeks back and I'm totally unhinged as a result. Would you like a snifter, seeing as you've already been condemned to the back seat?" George felt in his jacket pocket for the whisky flask. "Islay, single malt?"

"George! Not already! The evening is nowhere near started yet!" Carol complained.

"Och, it has now... Many thanks. That's real gentlemanly of ye." Duncan took the flask proffered and raised it in salute before tipping it back.

In the short drive to St Bart's, the two men on the back seat got on famously. Despite the fact that George was over a decade older than the younger man, Duncan could see they were kindred spirits. A few years between them, OK, but it looked like they had a similar taste in undomesticated women. He'd earlier been warned that George had something of a changeable nature but that was entirely acceptable. Under the influence of drink a certain fickleness of character was not exactly unknown for Duncan himself...though to say he always started fights was somewhat of an exaggeration. And to be offered a tipple of 10-year-old single malt within seconds of an introduction was no mean way to start a friendship. The car entered the uphill drive to St Bartholomew's College a few minutes later with the conversation inside beginning to get highly animated.

Sally lurched the motor to a halt rather precociously in the College Bursar's private parking spot. "Whoa! Steady, my girl," roared Duncan at the back. "Can't spill the amber nectar!" He clapped the top hurriedly down on to the whisky flask and passed it back to its owner.

Both sides of the Volvo opened up almost simultaneously and the four spilled noisily out in front of the large, oaken college doors. It was the first time George had got a look at what Carol was wearing as she emerged from the motor, and he had to look away almost at once. A long, black, clinging dress with deep V front and back that was far too dangerous to investigate closely if he didn't want to pass out straight away, with or without alcoholic encouragement. He quickly turned his attention to his immediate, inanimate, more sober-inducing surroundings.

"I say, I think I recognise this place!" said George, coming to a stop, stock still, facing the entrance in the middle of the parking lot. "Last time I was here I was in pyjamas!"

"I say, jolly good show, old sport!" cried Duncan, calling out in a fake English accent. "Fine place to go to sleep, what what?"

"Actually, Duncan, he claimed he had just woken up," said Carol, trying to steer both men off the tarmac and towards the way in to the college. "We never did get to the bottom of that. What do you say, George? How was it you were wandering around here in pyjamas?"

"All a bit of a blur, Carol. Can't explain it too well. Never happened before."

"Och, man, dinna disappoint me. Waking up in strange garb in strange places is summat I've done me whole life... Where ye taking me, woman?" Sally had now grabbed Duncan by the arm and was dragging him after George. She managed to quieten him down while they moved along the corridor and came to the door marked 'Senior Common Room'.

George was meanwhile reflecting upon his last visit to these environs. "As I recall, Carol, my attire was explained away to the college porter on that occasion as some sort of escapade in exper- imental psychology, am I right?"

"My God, George!" spluttered Duncan, just as the SCR door opened. "You're not one of those, surely!"

Dr Jonathan Adams, Master of St Bartholomew's, bowed very slightly as he welcomed four newly arrived guests to his college's Senior Common Room.

"Welcome ladies, gentlemen." He smiled graciously. "And may I enquire, sir – you are not one of *what*, if I may be so bold?" He looked at George.

"Hello, Dr Adams," Carol stepped in quickly. "Let me introduce you to George Potts and Duncan Mackay. Sally you know. Duncan is just recoiling from the discovery that George here is an experimental psychologist. Full of all sorts of tricks. Be careful he doesn't pull some sort of stunt on you tonight!"

"My goodness!"

"Dr Adams," George held out his hand, "pleased to make your acquaintance. Don't believe a word that your Student Welfare Officer tells you. She has a very fertile imagination and attracts all kinds of trouble. I wonder that the college is still standing after a year of her."

George stood tall, elegant, his paunch pulled in, looking every inch a respectable middle-aged professional – the dependable sort that banks, public offices and traditional universities are built around. The Master of St Bart's was instantly taken in and believed what he was told unquestioningly.

"My dear sir, you are quite correct. Miss Davies here has taken this college by storm and together with her colleague from Psychology, Miss Taylor, they have both had an equally seismic effect on the SCR. As you can see, the edifice is still standing but for how long we do not know. Welcome, welcome. Do come inside and meet my predecessor whose birthday we are celebrating tonight... And you, sir – Dr Mackay?"

"Aye, Dr Adams. I'm an old friend of Sally Taylor's. But in medicine, no experimental psychology – I canna say I trust any o' them, whether they be friends or no." He grinned as he entered the room and gave Sally a pinch on the bottom.

Sally winced and turned to look daggers at Duncan. George and Carol, meanwhile, advanced and met Mrs Bryony Adams who introduced them to Professor Geoffrey Collins and his wife Elizabeth.

"So, you are the new Welfare Officer, Carol," said Elizabeth Collins warmly. "So pleased to meet you – we've heard so much about you."

Carol smiled. "They say bad news travels fast. I hope it hasn't been too terrible."

"Not at all," said Professor Collins, taking an instant shine to this beautiful young woman. "Quite the contrary. We are delighted you seem to have settled in so well. And Dr Potts? An old acquaintance of Sally's?"

George was surprised to recognise these two. They were the people he had found breakfasting in the cottage near where he lived and where he had visited in his first outing as a greyhound. They had shared their sausages with him – how could he ever forget such an intimacy? Lovely people, he thought then – and now here they were: a very welcoming and friendly couple. They of course didn't know George.

"Old, certainly, but a relatively new acquaintance. Good evening to you both." George was genuinely pleased to meet them.

"George says he knows my dog better than he knows me, but I'm hoping this evening puts that matter right..."

"Really, my dear?" Professor Collins, a real ladies' man, put his arm through Carol's and at the same time turned to look at George. "And how is that, Dr Potts? Are you a dog lover?"

"Call me, George, please." He turned red at that question and looked away. His instantaneous thought was that he'd rather be a Carol lover but he had to calm down quickly. A more acceptable response was called for. "I can't say I love dogs, but they are the business, right enough. I observe dogs. And their owners. Their relationships are, er, fascinating…and Carol's greyhound is a lovely animal."

"There you are, Professor Collins – what did I say? He's more fascinated by my dog than by me…" She shot a fiery, challenging look at George as she said this. Again, George looked away.

"I'm quite sure you are wrong, my dear. He can see the same as me this evening – that you are perfectly gorgeous. I'm sure his interest in your dog is purely academic. An experimental psychologist? Not experimenting on dogs, surely, George?" Professor Collins frowned.

"Absolutely not, Professor." George was horrified. "I observe their behaviour. Very closely. I observe their owners' behaviour too. But I would never meddle or experiment with them, with neither in fact!" He shot a fiery glance back at Carol when he said that.

"Pleased to hear it, George. Don't take offence at my mistaken impression. I'm a zoologist – spent my life studying migration – retired now, of course, but I don't hold with experimenting on animals of any sort, domesticated or otherwise."

"Don't get him talking about it," warned Elizabeth. "I keep telling him I'll migrate if he doesn't ever stop!"

"We won't broach the subject again, Mrs Collins." George smiled at this kind, generous lady a few years his senior who didn't know he had met them both recently in another life. "We are as one on this subject so have no further need to discuss it."

"But your research sounds interesting, George. Don't let my dear wife stop you on that score. Any interesting results?"

"Well things are at an early stage as yet…"

"And we'll no go any further just now, either," came a Scottish voice, "or he'll be observing us next. No thanks, George. Professor Collins, how are ye? The name's Mackay, Duncan Mackay."

George was wondering what he was going to have to say, so Duncan's unknowing intervention had come to his rescue. More people were arriving now and seats in the common room were being taken. George found himself sat close to a coffee table with several glasses and a bottle of sherry waiting for attention. Bryony Adams, the Master's wife, came to see him.

"Sherry, George? Or would you like something a little stronger?" At that enquiry, George glanced across at Duncan, who looked meaningfully back from the next seat.

"Thank you, Mary. A little whisky perhaps?"

The First Lady of College was no slouch. She shimmered away and then was back in an instant clutching a bottle of Laphroaig. The sigh that emanated from Duncan as he saw her approach echoed his own feelings. This was looking like it might be a perfectly enjoyable evening.

A few sips of whisky later, when the SCR was almost full of guests, a gong sounded and the Master announced that dinner was to be served. A scrum of activity then took place as members present took to putting on academic gowns. George noticed to his horror that there was going to be some sort of procession to High Table, everyone gowned and flowing like a convention of Batmen and Batwomen. Except he had no gown.

Carol appeared magically by his side. "Don't worry, George," she breathed soothingly, "the SCR always keeps a number of gowns in reserve for guests who do not have one or have forgotten to bring them. I'll sort you out!" She slipped away through the crush and reappeared just as quickly.

Carol turned him around and slipped a gown over his shoulders, then turned him back and busied about, making sure everything fitted OK and his borrowed garment hung nicely. They stood very close together for a moment such that her perfume assaulted his nostrils. It was almost intimate. This sensuous being looked up at him, her eyes twinkling. George did his best to keep becalmed. It wasn't working. He could hardly avoid seeing that Carol's own gown was tastefully drawn about her but it could not quite conceal two glorious globes that had last made their acquaintance with his senses on the Northumberland coast, amongst the sand dunes, when she was bikini-clad and he was on four legs. Their impact on him now was much the same as then. In truth, he was delighted to be introduced to them again but wished he could bury his head somewhere. Preferably in her cleavage, he thought hotly. His head began to spin.

"Pull yourself together, George!" Carol's voice percolated through the red mists somehow. "You've been drinking too much already so steady on! No more! Now hang onto me and off we go..."

Couples drifted away out of the common room, two by two following each other, into the corridor outside, up a short flight of stairs and then to the SCR entrance to the dining hall. Traipsing up after them, almost at the rear of the procession, George couldn't help but think this was just like animals going up the gangplank following Noah into the Ark. Duncan and Sally were right behind him so George turned and let out a low moo. Duncan strangled a guffaw.

"George! Behave yourself!" Sally stared at him.

"Really, George! You're worse than a teenager!" Carol whispered fiercely.

The line of guests for High Table entered the dining hall and moved around to find their places – each individually named – whilst the gathered numbers of students all stood to attention and waited. It was all very dignified. Then the President of the JCR came forward and recounted out loud the grace in Latin, very prettily done, before everyone took their seats and each table instantly erupted in conversation. Waitresses came forward and circulated the first dish, soup, while bottles on each table were passed around and a choice of red or white wines was offered to all.

George looked about him, taking it all in. It really was a most civilised gathering. How things change. *Last time I was here*, he thought, *I was rushing crazily from end to end, with porters and students running after me, and I was crashing about, upending breakfast on one table after another.* He was glad no one else knew that but he.

George's attention was brought back to High Table and the people either side and opposite. He was seated between Carol and Sally; Professor Collins, the ex-Master, was diagonally across the table and next to his wife, but smack in front of George was someone else he now recognised. He was a handsome enough fellow: possessing sun-tanned, striking features; he wore glasses and had the air of someone who thought himself important. It was the man George had last seen in a Barbour jacket walking his two Dalmatians. It was a certain Dr Jordan Humphries and he was trying to make conversation with Carol, whom he recognised from that day of the dog display.

"So you're the new Welfare Officer here are you? And how's student welfare?" He smiled and flashed his eyes at Carol but showed as much interest in this profession as the plate of soup which he left to go cold in front of him.

"Ooh, I'm trying to give them as many problems as I can," Carol answered sarcastically. She could see the sort he was – handsome, and he knew it. She had had years of experience of this type.

"And I'm sure you're very successful too," he rejoined. "What's your background?"

"Psychology, Edinburgh," Carol sniffed. *Bloody nerve*, she thought. *What right has he got to go prying into my background on a social occasion such as this?* "What's yours?"

"Geophysics, Cambridge." Humphries grinned. "That's a real science, not a pseudo-science!"

George exploded. "Pseudo-science? Good grief! I've seen more pseuds in geophysics than I've ever seen in psychology!" He was not going to have this dog castrator insult his partner for the evening.

"Have you, indeed?" The arrogant geophysicist was unmoved. "And you're the experimental psychologist? I haven't seen you here before."

"I haven't seen you either," George replied sweetly. This was a lie of course – the last time he had seen him, Jordan Humphries was rolling around in dog dung. It suited him, George thought.

"Are you at Durham?" Humphries was still pushing, wanting to see if George could be labelled, categorised, and thus dispensed with.

"Nope." George wasn't going to make it easy for him. "Private practice. Nothing pseud. I see real people and animals. Lots of *amazing* behaviour. Not inanimate rocks…"

"Well, my friend, inanimate rocks yield the most *amazing* secrets to scientific enquiry. Just how many secrets can your pseudo-science reveal, eh? Just exactly what predictive power does experimental psychology possess?"

Professor Geoffrey Collins could see the sparks just beginning to fly here and thought he'd better defuse the situation. "Well, what you've been researching recently sounds interesting, George, want to tell us something about it?"

Carol and Sally were privately scared. George was getting well out of his depth in this university milieu and that bastard across the table would absolutely wallow in triumph if he could strip away George's cover and reveal him for the imposter that he actually was.

George was not going to back down, however. His girl had been insulted by that strutting cockerel opposite and now the Barboured Bantam was crowing that his work was more scientific and far superior to anything that George could offer. Well, there were a couple of aces George reckoned he could play if he could just shift the conversation in the right direction.

"Ahem, Professor Collins, you know it's said that people get to look like their pets over time? Well I'm not so sure. But there is, I believe, some interesting correlations you can pursue about the types of people and the types of dogs they have…"

"Och, man…like they say about people and the cars they drive?" Duncan inclined his head on the other side of Sally and looked along at George. He wasn't about to leave him to go it alone in the head-to-head contest that he could see was coming.

"Yes, yes," said Jordan Humphries feigning indifference. "Boring accountants trying to compensate by driving E-type Jags, that sort of thing…"

Carol almost choked on her meal. She took a sip of wine to wet her throat and then slipped a hand down to squeeze George on the thigh. She wanted to tell him that this accountant didn't need a flash motor to compensate for anything.

"Well, there's all sorts of anecdotal evidence about that, of course," George was getting into his stride. "We can have a look at that in a bit, if you like, but that wouldn't satisfy our geophysicist here. Not rigorous enough."

George waved his hand in Jordan Humphries' direction. The said scientist grimaced like a dead fish. George was holding centre stage now, had captured most of the table's attention and he had just anticipated his adversary's main criticism, leaving him little room to regain the initiative.

"No, cars are not my field of enquiry…" George harrumphed. He'd got the hang of this academic talk and was going to ram it down the throat of his rival opposite. "*My* interest was actually awoken by observing the greyhound of my partner for this evening – the lovely Carol…"

All eyes swivelled around to look at the lovely Carol. She was certainly an eyeful, and most people on High Table enjoyed looking at her – though George held his head aside, looking nowhere in particular whilst he was marshalling his thoughts. Carol meanwhile was holding her breath. It was like when she watched George as a greyhound – knowing that there was some stunt he was going to pull and no observer knew it, only her. But she couldn't for the life of her guess what he was up to.

"Carol's greyhound is a very well-behaved, somewhat passive and very cooperative female. A lovely dog. Her owner is equally lovely, of course, but her character is the opposite in every other way..."

"George, that is too much!" Carol blustered whilst others around the table began to laugh. Carol was clearly well–known and liked by many of the SCR. "You're implying that I'm badly behaved and uncooperative?"

"I wouldn't put it that way myself...but certainly highly active and...and *untamed*, shall we say?"

"What a nerve you have, George Potts!" Carol protested. She was smiling, however, albeit she still didn't know what his game was.

"Well said, sir! I entirely agree. And her colleague is the same. Sally and Carol in the same house as their poor greyhound. No wonder that dog is like she is!" Duncan raised his wine glass. "Here's to experimental psychology!" There was more laughter at that.

"Come, come, sir. This is hardly science. One dog's behaviour contrasting with its owner, or owners? You cannot convince anyone with such paltry evidence." Humphries was determined to ridicule this whole charade.

"I quite agree, quite agree. My, um, hypothesis is not based on just this case, however. I have been observing dogs for some little time now, quite closely. And there are definitely some firm conclusions that are possible. Not in all cases, you understand. There are so many variables to take into account. But if you look at some people apart from their animals, and some animals apart from their owners, one can make some pretty safe predictions about the behaviours concerned..."

Humphries immediately seized upon the opening offered by this remark. Here was an opportunity to make this so-called experimental psychologist look the complete idiot he took him to be.

"Safe predictions? I'll bet you cannot make even one. I reckon there are a number of dog owners around this table – apart from guesswork, you try and tell me the sort of dogs they have. You won't be able to!"

"Well that is something of a tall order, my friend, since I know no one here very well, except for the company I came with…I have observed no behaviour of anyone present – apart, I suppose, from yourself and Professor Collins, whom I met just now in the SCR."

"Well we are two people to start with. Both dog owners, as it happens. Come on – give us your scientific prediction. Put your money where your mouth is…what sort of dogs do we have? £50 if you can get even near one of them. £100 for both. I'll gladly pay that to you if you can do it, and you pay me if you cannot. How's that?"

"Dr Humphries! That is really most unfair of you. Dr Potts here knows little of either of us…" Professor Collins was anxious to try and stop these two adversaries from locking horns.

Carol looked round at George and put an arm on his shoulder as if to restrain him. "George, be careful…you don't have to do this," she whispered. At the same time she was beginning to see where this was going. George only looked back and winked.

"I'll take on his bet. Please do not concern yourself, Geoffrey." George affected the familiar address to the ex-Master of St Bart's. He figured he was a friend now and wanted to show him he felt that. "I'll take up this challenge since I've been so bold as to say that my science will stand up to scrutiny…and so – my money is on the table." George fished out his wallet and placed it unopened in front of him. He knew well enough that he only had around £20 in it, but the gesture was convincing. Everyone's eyes were upon him.

Elizabeth Collins began openly protesting – she was asserting that this was not a fair contest and urged her husband to stop this. That was an interesting reaction. George took note.

Jordan Humphries was meanwhile sitting opposite with a gleam in his eye and his ruddy face smiling broadly. George had an idea that he was being set up...but he wasn't going to fall for it. Like a poker player with a full hand, he also had something he could call upon that he reckoned would beat his opponent.

"Dr Humphries," George began, "unlike the natural sciences like with your study of rocks, the study of humankind deals with very much more unpredictable data. Nonetheless I insist that some really quite remarkable correlations do indeed hold. Looking at how some people behave you can begin to read them, as they say, like a book. But in the case of your own challenge to gauge the nature of Professor Collins dog therefore, I'll say this: I think you are trying to trick me..."

George watched the man's reaction. Was there a perceptible change in expression? George was not a man who had ever played poker before so his powers of observation and of interpreting an opponent's deadpan face were nowhere near as good as he was claiming. He was now a long way out on a limb in this contest and there was no route back. He plunged on.

"My money is on the table, sir, and, based partly on your own behaviour, my guess is that Professor Collins does not have a dog. No dog at all. But I bet that he did have one *once*, however, and that it was a dearly-loved animal. And what type of dog? I'll bet that it was no pedigree hound, but a simple, everyday, ordinary mongrel of a dog that loved its owners as surely as its owners loved it. And now? I'd say that Professor Collins and his wife, kind folk and dog-less that they are, will on occasions shower their affection for the canine species on just about every stray and adventurous hound that that they encounter in their retirement. How's that? That is my prediction, sir, based on what I have seen of your own reactions and the little I have observed of the character of this most distinguished couple tonight!"

Elizabeth Collins gave a shout. Not quite loud enough to cross the dining hall because the meal was well underway and the students, with wine now loosening their tongues, were making the very devil of a racket. But everyone on High Table heard her and she added to her cry by gleefully clapping her hands. Professor Geoffrey Collins was at the same time grinning from ear to ear and he finally gave voice to his feelings.

"By God, sir! That is the best, most deserving £50 I've ever seen earned in all my life. In fact, I'd go so far as to say I'll match that £50 of yours Jordon, with a note of the same value myself. Tremendous! Your prediction was absolutely correct in every detail. In every detail, George, old fellow. You are a marvel! An absolute marvel."

Carol simply beamed at George. She put her hand across and squeezed his thigh again. She didn't know how he had done it. He must have known something – she realised he was too artful a character to have gone into that completely cold – but she reckoned there was nonetheless a fair bit of guesswork involved as well.

Duncan thumped the table and then raised his glass again. "Hats off to the psychologist! Hurrah! One in the eye for the geophysie…the geophysys…the man with the red face! Aye, sir. That got you, didn't it!" Duncan was clearly getting well-oiled and enjoying this evening a little more at every passing minute. "C'mon, George! Now give us the other dog! The one this pseud says he owns…"

A buzz of excited conversation swept around the table and came to rest finally with the two men at the heart of the contest looking keenly at each other. One was red-faced, sour-faced and clearly rattled. The rather underhand ruse he had tried to pull – picking out a dog owner who had no dog – had not worked. He didn't know how his opponent had rumbled it but he was now hoping that this man would not do it again. The other, of course, was by far the more composed of the two and gave off an air of quiet confidence. Carol was now grinning inside. This time she knew that George could not lose.

"Well, ladies, gentlemen, like I say, there are correlations that can be made with dogs and owners. Some correlations are not always that close such is the nature of the variables one finds. Sometimes, to be honest, there has to be a fair degree of guesstimate involved – like in the case of the Collins' dog, I have to confess. I own that I was lucky to get every detail right on that one. But in this next case of the geophysicist sitting in front of me, his character, the evidence of the man, is so strong that I feel there is no need for guesswork at all...just a matter of extrapolating what I see in front of me. Dr Humphries – I bet you do not have one dog. I'll bet you have at least two. And I'll bet they are two pedigree hounds, really showy, prize possessions – prize pets fit to grace the living room of your undoubtedly showy home and the undoubtedly grand, gas-guzzling motor, probably a four-by-four, which you own..."

The face of George's rival across the table was now a complete picture. Red and fizzing. Someone shouted: "Well done! You've got the motor! Now – what breed for the dogs? What are they like?"

George continued. "The two dogs I have deduced he possesses will be docile, thoroughly tamed. The dog castrated; the bitch spayed. They will be extremely well-behaved and will pose no competition for their owner. What breed? Does it matter? Pedigree, of course: dogs that have to look good. What do you reckon? Dalmatians? Pointers? Great Danes?" There was a rising murmur of noise about the table. "Hmmm, two dogs I said. Yes, I can hear you saying it already. Dalmatians! How's that?"

Dr Jordan Humphries jumped up, incensed. "I don't believe any of this! These are party tricks. This is not science! You've cheated! Your woman here has put you up to it! She's given you inside information!"

"Why, you...you...common *scumbag*!" Carol couldn't control her language, she was so shocked. "You insult me just because you can't stand losing…"

Humphries was still standing, leaning over the table with his colour and his temper rising. "This is some sort of scam you people pull. It's all a stunt…you cheats…"

He got no further. With a "Hey, Jordie, catch this!" Duncan leaped to his feet and swung a fist across into the other's face. Dr Jordan Humphries was catapulted back into his chair which promptly tipped over under the impact and deposited the limp, semi-conscious body onto the floor behind the table.

Chapter 14

Conversation around High Table ceased immediately. Knives and forks were frozen in movement. Mouths stopped in mid-chew. The great majority of the students in the body of the dining hall had not noticed the swift, aerial departure of Dr Jordan Humphries from both consciousness and his four-course meal but the members of the SCR seated all round and about him had certainly seen, and heard, his explosive send-off. George thought he'd better switch attention away from his Scottish friend and ally who was just resuming his seat whilst wiping a trace of geophysical blood from his fist.

"Oh dear! Now there's an interesting case in migration to study, Geoffrey." George looked across at the retired Professor Collins. "The sudden flight of the species scumbag..."

Stunned at first like all the others, Professor Geoffrey Collins nodded with a faint, barely perceptible smile, looking down beside him at the figure sprawled on the floor which was now uttering a low groan. At the scumbag reference, meanwhile, Carol was profuse with apologies.

"I...I'm so sorry for using that language. Really...but he was outrageous, accusing me of cheating...of being involved in some deceit to trick him out of his money... Please forgive me!" Carol looked pleadingly at the Master, Dr Adams, begging his pardon.

"Nothing to apologise for, beautiful," George intervened. "The brute was completely out of order, insulting you just because he couldn't get the better of me. Dreadful behaviour!"

"Aye, dinna apologise, Carol," Duncan spoke up. "Ye did nothing wrong. But I think I should clear up the mess that I've created... With your permission, ladies, gentlemen..." Duncan rose again from the table, bowed to the Master and ex-Master and walked quickly around to the other side and bent down to catch hold of the concussed geophysicist. He dragged him smartly back and out of the serving door behind which led down to the kitchens. Despite the considerable intake of alcohol Duncan had imbibed so far he was the fastest to seize control of the situation and restore the High Table to some semblance of normality, although now with two gaps in the line of guests at dinner. And the body that was being dragged away only bumped twice into the wall and the door jamb on the way out: quite an efficient removal job, considering that Duncan, bent double and looking backwards, was by this time having just a little trouble with his vision.

All of the others at High Table were still struck dumb and didn't quite know how to react to this astonishing and highly irregular turn of events. Fisticuffs were hardly common amongst members of the Senior Common Room. Dr Jonathan Adams, Master of St Barts, thought he had better say something but struggled to find anything coherent to help move the evening's discourse along.

"Ahem...Dr Potts...that was an impressive display of, er, psychology you've just demonstrated... Not some party trick as...as has been alleged?"

"Indeed not, Dr Adams. I regret that our absent friend had the nerve to challenge a fellow on his active research project and as a result he came out a sore loser, as your Welfare Officer quite rightly pointed out."

"Quite so, George," offered Geoffrey Collins. "I must say that I've never, in all my years here as Master before Jonathan, never *ever* heard one member of the SCR dare to disparage the field of expertise of another. Quite, quite unacceptable."

"Riding to a fall, you might say?" suggested Elizabeth Collins with a grin.

George loved her for that comment. "Well, it was rather foolhardy of him to tackle me on my own grounds, so to speak. I would never have had the arrogance to challenge his own research findings..."

Carol was still upset. "He insinuated that I was colluding with you, George, in some cheap stunt to bring him down." She looked around at the others at High Table "The trouble is, I *did* see him out walking his Dalmatians a week or so ago and I guess he recognised me this evening...but I never spoke about that with George here at any time since. I really didn't, I do assure you."

"Even if you had done, my dear, given that he had seen you with his dogs before then it was even more foolish of the man to issue the challenge he did to your colleague here. He brought it on himself, after all. It was not George's idea to enter into the wager." Professor Collins was not prone to criticise attractive young women who brought poise and pleasure to his table when it was another who was guilty of a serious academic *faux pas*.

"Did you get any money out of the man before he was despatched, George?" Elizabeth Collins asked.

"No, no." George picked up his wallet from beside his plate and re-pocketed it. "He, um, didn't have time to pay up before leaving... But it doesn't matter. I don't want his money."

By this time the buzz of conversation around High Table had restarted as others joined in with comments between themselves and various apologies were made to waiters and waitresses who moved in and out to tidy up and clear away debris that the absent geophysicist had spilt in his hurry to depart. George noted with some pleasure that the college staff could scarcely contain their amusement at what had transpired and there was no doubt that, for them, this evening's entertainment had surpassed anything that had been witnessed here for many years. No doubt what had happened would be actively discussed and would pass quickly around the university circuit like wildfire – between staff and students, Senior and Junior Common Rooms, colleges and departments, indeed half the population of Durham city.

Duncan Mackay M.D. reappeared through the service door

and quietly enquired of the Master if he might continue with his meal. Whatever else might be thought of the man, George realised, fiery Scot and fond of the juice as he was, having taken one errant guest out of circulation he was careful now to observe decorum and not disturb matters any further. The Master, caught still wondering whether or not he ought to make some fuss about this Caledonian laying out one of his guests, in the end thought it best not to draw any further attention to him than was necessary.

Duncan returned to the table. Sally rose to greet her partner as he moved round to take his place again. She gave him a quick kiss. George nodded and signalled his pleasure at seeing his ally come back.

"Well, Doctor, how's the patient?" he enquired. Many others looked up to catch the response.

"Och, he'll live, though I think his jaw'll need an X-ray. I left him sleeping in the lobby, waiting for the ambulance to pick him up."

The buzz of conversation reached a new high. Despite everyone looking at him, Duncan wasted no further time in tucking into his meal – his appetite quite stimulated by his exertions. He couldn't stop smiling as he shovelled down mouthfuls of steak and potatoes.

The rest of the meal passed off relatively smoothly. The Master was concerned to lead small talk away from lingering on this wholly unfortunate episode and preferred to introduce some discussion about the university's building plans, the expansion of college numbers, the calendar of events at the end of the academic year, indeed on just about anything other than the embarrassment for him of SCR members engaged in a public brawl. Sally, sitting opposite him, an astute female and professional psychologist into the bargain, wanted to reassure Dr Adams that the efficient manner of Dr Humphries' departure had in fact caused no great disturbance to the evening's proceedings and was anyway more to be welcomed than to have the man's provocative presence continuing amongst the members of the SCR for the rest of the evening. She was, of course, not an entirely unbiased observer of what had occurred.

The whole purpose of the Formal Dinner was, it must be remembered, for the college to welcome the return of Professor Geoffrey Collins, the previous Master, to St Bart's; to celebrate his birthday, and to offer him the opportunity to say a few words of goodbye and best wishes to the graduating class of students whom he had once welcomed on their admission to this university institution three years earlier. This central objective of the evening's gathering asserted itself as soon as the meal came to a close. Directly SCR members had finished eating and dessert and coffees had been cleared away, Professor Collins rose to his feet, came round from behind High Table and stood at the head of the dining hall, in front of the students who now all waited in silence for his final address.

George was most impressed by the quiet, dignified manner of this kindly gentleman and the warmth and consideration he showed to the undergraduates assembled before him as this ex-Master spoke of the pleasure he had had in serving the college and how he hoped these students, his last students at Durham, would all go out into the world the better for sharing their formative years with him in this place. A storm of applause and various cries of appreciation from all quarters met his remarks. It was an emotional moment for the retired professor. Geoffrey Collins turned and even wiped a tear from his face as he waved goodbye to his students and then he led the guests at High Table away to his right, out of the dining hall and back downstairs towards the Senior Common Room. George, as before, was towards the back of the procession and now, for the first time, began to see the life of certain academics at the university as something more than just being surrounded by stuffed shirts and pompous old bores.

George's own contribution to the evening, with the able support of Duncan Mackay, had also been far from the stereotype that he had previously held of life up in the clouds of academe. Clearly he had to reassess his opinion of what went on within the walls of university buildings. He was thinking these thoughts all the way down the staircase and along the corridor below before Carol slipped her arm through his and drew him aside just as he was about to re-enter the Senior Common Room. She held onto him until all the others had passed and they were left alone outside the SCR door. Then she threw her arms around his neck, pulled his head down towards her and kissed him full on the lips, her eyes glittering.

"George, you were absolutely *amazing* up there. Wonderful! My knight in shining armour."

George froze. The confident manner in which he had been conducting himself up until now suddenly deserted him.

"I've never see you like that before," Carol continued, "you were brilliant. You leapt to my defence and absolutely demolished that bastard."

"No…no…Duncan did that." George shook his head, trying to calm his nerves.

"I don't mean physically. I mean verbally, intellectually, emotionally – you outshone him in every way. You wiped the floor with him."

George couldn't look at her. She was the one who was shining and he couldn't cope with it. His pulse was racing and he wanted to turn and stare at the wall to control himself. He tried to focus on the man he had outwitted rather than this beautiful young woman that was pressing her body against his. Unfortunately, his hormones wouldn't let him. And Carol wasn't letting go.

"It was…it wasn't…so easy, I mean, so difficult…Christ, Carol, get off me!"

"No!" She kissed him again. George nearly fainted.

The SCR door opened and someone was coming out. Carol

quickly removed her arms, stepped back and smoothed her dress down. She span round to meet whoever it was about to emerge beside her. She needn't have worried. It was Sally.

"I wondered where you two'd got to," Sally said. She saw Carol smiling demurely and George looking perfectly uncomfortable, sweating profusely, and instantly understood what was going on. She joined in with the attack.

"George, that was a tremendous show upstairs! Has Carol thanked you sufficiently yet? If not, I'll add my congratulations."

"Be my guest, Sal." Carol waved her forward. George burbled incoherently as Sally planted another kiss on his lips.

"Aye, man, ye deserve that," a Scottish voice said. Duncan had followed Sally out into the corridor and, like his partner, quickly took in the embarrassment of one so deserving, yet so unused to receiving praise and affection when it was due. "It was well done, sah. Ye turned the man inside oot, and showed him to be the blustering idiot he was."

George by this time was leaning against the wall, trying to hold himself up. He was thoroughly unaccustomed to having sensual young women showering him with kisses.

"And, Duncan, you also deserve your reward," Carol turned and embraced him. It was kisses all round.

"Well thankye very much, Carol." He licked his lips. "Much appreciated!"

"Can we go inside now?" George's voice had returned to him and, released from his torture while Carol's attention was elsewhere, he took the opportunity to run for cover. The Senior Common Room beckoned.

Tables in the SCR had been set up with bottles of port, glasses and a variety of cheeses whilst the Formal Dinner had been underway and Bryony Adams, the Master's wife, was busy ensuring all SCR guests were being served. Seeking refuge, George made straight for the first table and armed himself with a glass in one hand, a plate of cheese in the other. He then wandered over to the furthest corner to escape attention. Armchairs were dotted around the room and arranged in several circles so that guests could chat amiably enough with each other in groups of four or five. George's attempt to retreat into anonymity was not successful, however. Carol came after him.

"It's no good, I'm not going to leave you alone." She pushed George into one armchair and took the one next to it. "And you have to *look* at me! Don't try and pretend I'm not here."

George looked at her, as commanded. It was the look of a trapped animal. Carol softened.

"You were absolutely on top of your game upstairs, George. So confident and assured and you took that bastard apart. Can't you relax with me now? Please?"

The trouble was, George admitted to himself, that Carol was looking absolutely stunning and it was excruciatingly painful looking at her. He would love to let himself go and fall in love with her. But he was a middle-aged old dodderer, married to a dragon, employed in a dull office, living a boring life and the only excitement he could offer this vivacious and sparkling young beauty was to metamorphose on occasions into a quadruped. What a sad case that was! In contrast, milling around behind Carol was a room full of interesting people who were engaged in undoubtedly fascinating careers and could keep up an intellectual and diverting conversation for more than the fifteen minutes of so that he could bluster on about, providing no one knew him. What was he doing here and what was she doing bothering with him?

George could say nothing. Looking at her, his eyes actually started welling up.

Carol rose from her chair, took a pace forward and bent over George as he was sitting there transfixed. Her perfume washed over him in waves. Her beautiful breasts were hovering inches from his face. She lowered her head and gently kissed his forehead.

"Christ, George! You are a lovely, *lovely* man. I'm going to leave you for a bit but I'm not leaving you for long…OK?" She moved gracefully away.

Sally was standing by one of the tables, sipping port and talking to Duncan. She saw Carol approach.

"What do you think of this big hunk, Carol? I think I might just marry him after that show on High Table. Bang! He certainly knows how to make an impact!"

Duncan grinned. "Well, lassie, I must have proposed to ye a dozen times and got nowhere. I have tried being gentlemanly to a fault, with no success. The first time I smack some bastard in the face in front of ye, y'go all amorous on me. I should've taken ye out on a Saturday night in Inverness wi'me many years ago. We'd be married wi a dozen bairns by now!"

Carol laughed. "There are as many ways to a women's heart as there are women in the world, Duncan. You've just got to figure out which way suits the woman you want."

"And it's our job to keep you guessing," said Sally. "Though I think I might have given the game away now."

Carol smiled. She was pleased to see these two enjoying each other's company. But it only reinforced the difficulty she was experiencing with the one whose company she wanted.

"Sal, take a look at that man of mine behind me, sitting in the corner," Carol whispered. "What do you reckon?"

"He looks sad. And alone. What's going on?"

"I've got to get him to come out of his shell…but he won't, not in here. What am I going to do?"

"I'll go see him; nee bother!" Duncan grabbed a bottle of port, left the girls behind and went over to join his newfound friend. He topped up George's glass and refilled his own. George looked up gratefully as the Scotsman settled down in the chair Carol had vacated. He relaxed with an audible sigh.

"Aaah. Thanks, Duncan. That's what I need."

"Aye. Port or whisky. I'm partial to both."

"Me too. One's quicker but both have their attractions." George pecked at a slice of cheese and chewed it slowly, savouring its taste to contrast with the last sip of port. He leaned back and stretched out his legs; his pulse slowing, his colour at last beginning to recede.

"Och, man, this is the life: plenty o' drink, good-looking women, and nothing like punching the lights out o' some mean Sassenach who thinks he's so damn superior."

George laughed. "Thanks, Duncan. You're the real deal. Even makes me think I should move north of the border."

"Nay, man. We'd no have ye. Pyschologists should stay well away. Look – we kicked out those two girls yonder, no matter they're gorgeous to look at."

"I see. Would you have accountants then?"

"More people after our money? Like as not. Are ye trained in accounts as well, George?"

"Sort of. Actually I don't want any of your country's money, nor am I interested in its psychology…but I could do with some of the space you've got. And the mountains. And the single malt."

"Aye, we've plenty o' all that ye can enjoy. D'ye have the flask wi' ye still?"

With glasses of port now drained, the two men passed the flask between them and conversation lapsed into the slow appreciation of 10-year-old Islay. Professor Geoffrey Collins, enjoying his birthday and not wishing it to end as various guests now began to take their leave, saw these two relaxing in the corner and so wandered across to share their company and see what they were up to. He brought the bottle of Laphroaig with him.

"Good evening, gentlemen, may I join you?" He was a polite as always.

George sat up. "Hello, Geoffrey, please do. There's a bottle of port around here somewhere and I have a flask of single malt in addition to what you are carrying. What'll you have?"

"The port'll do fine for now, thank you. Well, George, you got the measure of me and my affection for dogs quickly enough. How'd you do it?"

"Not so difficult if you know dogs as well as I do." George did not wish to elaborate. He reached for the Laphroaig.

Over the next fifteen minutes, as the common room began to thin out, the three men in the corner settled into discussion and began to explore their common interests – women, whisky, animals. Duncan asked George if he could guess what creature he kept.

"I'd say you were a cat person, Duncan. Someone who appreciates independence; a sense of wild, untameable nature. Also, they're not so much bother to keep!"

"Got it in one! Ye have a reel canny knack aboot thee, mon!" The accent was becoming broader and broader with each passing whisky.

George grinned. He told Duncan that he would be sure to appreciate Mr Tibbs, a real degenerate feline neighbour of his. The Scotsman agreed that that was most likely.

At the sound of the SCR door opening, Geoffrey Collins looked round, albeit with a little difficulty. Jonathan Adams and his wife were leaving and so the professor called out merrily to say cheerio. Only Carol, Sally, Elizabeth Collins and the three men in the corner were hanging on until midnight. It was clear that the Master and his wife wished to say their farewells and leave them to it.

George, Duncan and Geoffrey Collins all drained their glasses, rose as one and went to say goodbye. Of the three of them, George's head was now definitely feeling the worst for the effects of a mix of alcohol so as soon as he had shaken hands with the departing Master and Mrs Adams he staggered quickly back to his seat.

Meanwhile, like the three men, Carol, Sally and Elizabeth were enjoying themselves together as each was finding out more about each other. They had just started laughing about the foibles of their various menfolk when Carol turned to see what was happening in the corner.

"Oh no! *George!*"

Duncan and Geoffrey Collins turned away from the door to see what Carol was concerned about. They both stopped in surprise.

"Have I just seen what I think I've seen...or am I hallucinating?" asked Duncan.

"I think I've seen what you've just seen and I'm thinking the same as you," answered Professor Collins.

"George, *NO!*" Carol was beside herself. She did so want to get to know this man who she was desperately fond of.

"Is this experimental psychology, d'ye reckon?" asked Duncan

"Testing if seeing is believing, do you mean?" the professor replied

Carol rushed over to where George had been sitting and was now talking to a large black greyhound with a white bib. An elegant-looking animal, though with a somewhat dazed expression in its eyes.

"Maybe this is a test in seeing how far can you go in manipulating the environment before people lose faith in who they are and where they are," suggested Duncan. "Present people with something preposterous and impossible, and see how long it takes for them to go crazy...I've heard of such experiments. Even thought of doing one or two myself a while back."

"Not normally carried out in Senior Common Rooms, though," said the ex-Master of St Barts. "Not very scientific, in my opinion. Another whisky, my friend?"

"Don't mind if I do," agreed Duncan. "Yep, too many variables you canna control here...unless o' course this whole place is rigged up for it and we're the guinea pigs, specially selected. Come to think of it, the invitation for tonight's dinner was conveyed to me by a couple of very suspicious psychologists..."

"Not so in my case," ruminated Professor Collins, peering carefully into his glass. "And it was I who asked for the company of the two psychologists I believe you are referring to. Of course they could have captured the whole occasion and twisted it to serve their own evil ends. Do you think they might have done that?"

"Do you mind, you two?" Carol was getting annoyed. "We're confronted with a serious and upsetting animal transformation here and you two drunks are carrying on an academic conversation of no merit whatsoever!"

Sally and Elizabeth backed up this outburst with supportive cries of their own, demanding their partners behave themselves. It was having no effect.

"Pychologists! I wouldn't trust 'em as far as I could throw 'em. In fact, I'm planning to marry one of them as a means of tying her down and exercising some degree of control over her..."

"Risky strategy, old boy. Very risky. Had you thought it might be you that ends up being tied down?"

There was a sudden, sharp bark from Greyhound George that stopped all conversation short. Then Geoffrey Collins put his hand up to his mouth.

"That *is* a dog! Not a hallucination."

"Ha, ha, bloody ha!" Carol shot a withering look at the professor.

"Not only is that a dog, but I think I recognise it. Elizabeth – do you recognise it?" Professor Geoffrey Collins, ex-Master of St Bart's and one who knew the college inside and out, was beginning to put things into their proper perspective.

"Yes, dear. That dog came to see us once. You were impressed with his appreciation of the television. We fed him sausages."

George wuffed in agreement.

Carol was not placated. She ignored everyone else, caught hold of George's head in her hands and searched his doggy eyes.

"I'm really, really upset with you, do you realise that? I so much wanted to share this whole evening with you; get to know you better. Do you understand?" It was her turn for her eyes to fill up now. "George – how can you keep on running away from me? Just as soon as you show me something lovely about you, just as soon as I begin to get close to you, you do this to me! It's so unfair!"

George wuffed sorrowfully.

"Stop it, George! Turn right back. Go on! Do it."

George's big eyes looked back at Carol. He gently shook his head. He couldn't do it. Carol promptly burst into tears.

Sally came forward to console her friend. "I think we ought to take George home, Carol," she said. "We'll go too and leave him 'til he sorts himself out. Nothing more we can do."

Carol nodded dumbly. She searched for a tissue to dry her face.

"I think this means goodnight, Professor," Duncan volunteered. "It's been a real pleasure meeting you. G'night, Mrs Collins."

"Goodnight all of you," replied Geoffrey Collins. He and his wife shook hands with Duncan and embraced the two girls. "It certainly has been most enjoyable meeting you at last, Carol, Sally, and I hope this won't be the last time. Do, er, give my best wishes to George when he is feeling more his old self again."

Carol regained her composure. "I've no need to tell him, he understands you quite well, Professor Collins. He might look different but he is still the same *most frustrating individual*!" She fired a venomous look at George. "But thank you. I have greatly enjoyed your company and that of Elizabeth too, so I'm sure we'll meet again."

They all went outside and parted company in the parking bay. Sally opened up the Volvo. Carol insisted that Duncan go in front so that she could share the last few moments with Greyhound George on the back seat. George was thoroughly subdued by this time. They all went back to George's place first of all and Carol opened the door for him to get out. George really wanted to say goodbye and thanks, but after a quick bark in the car and a poke of Duncan's back he could do no more. Carol was too upset to speak to him so he leapt out and ran off quickly down the back lane towards the garages. It was good to exercise his legs in the open air. He let rip with a few loud barks to clear his head and release the built-up frustration inside of him at how the evening had finished. He then cantered to a stop outside his garage and checked that, yes, he had left it open enough to get a paw inside and pull. Wriggling his head under, he then heaved the door up enough for him to crawl inside. He found the old overcoat and also some foam rubber he had placed in the corner for just such an occasion as this, so he quickly got himself settled for the rest of the night. It would be a different day in the morning.

Chapter 15

Annabel Potts had just come back upstairs to her bedroom when she heard a dog bark. She was paralysed on the spot. It was a bark she recognised. A short, sharp venomous bark that turned her stomach over and her insides to water. It sounded from outside, from where she had once been chased from Stephen Maxwell's house to this. There were some street lights out the back, illuminating the garages, and there trotting along in front of them was that vicious black monster that had terrorised her and that she wished dead. Dead as a moon-rock and preferably as distant. She reached for her mobile.

"Stevie?"

"Yes, my love? You back OK? George still away?"

"Yes, yes, no problem. Quick! Go and look out the back window. By the garages. Can you see what I can see?"

"By God, Annabel. It's that dog! Yeah – I can see it alright. What's it doing?"

"Good question. Keep looking. It...it seems to be scrabbling about our garage. Of all the nerve! It had better not pee on the door there... No... No. Look! It's trying to get in..."

"Annabel! Would you believe it! It *is* getting in. It's found its way under the door. It's, it's *gone!*" Stephen Maxwell saw the whiplash tail of the greyhound disappear into the garage.

"Stevie! We can trap it there. Quick – out you go. Shut the door down after it. It'll never get out!"

Stephen Maxwell put the phone in the breast pocket of his pyjamas and ran downstairs. Annabel stood guard at the window and watched him appear in slippers in his garden, hurry up the path to the back gate and from there, disappearing for a moment behind the tall garden walls and the next-door neighbour's shed, he ran along the lane outside to the garages. The evil black dog had not reappeared in all that time so Stephen got to the Potts garage and slammed the door down tight. Annabel almost jumped out of her skin in delight. She pulled a dressing gown around her shoulders and hurried down as well to meet her lover, with whom she had spent most of the evening already, outside on the lane in front of the garages. They both hopped up and down with glee and, not caring who might see them, embraced under the lamppost.

"Got the blighter!" said Smarmy Stephen.

"Oh, well done, my love! He can't get out now. There's no other way in or out but by this door."

"Have you got the key so we can lock him in?"

"No, George keeps it with all the others for the house on his key ring, but it doesn't matter. No dog can open the door from the inside once the catch is engaged. That poisonous wolf can push all he likes but it will never open."

"Right. Well, now you can sleep soundly tonight, my love. I'll phone my man in the farm to come down tomorrow morning bright and early and collar the bugger. He'll either drag it out and do the business in his van, or take the gun in and finish him off inside. Either way we'll be rid of him. George isn't going to take out his Land Rover early in the morning is he?"

"Not likely. He isn't back yet and I expect he'll not get up in the morning until relatively late. And then I guess he'll take a slow breakfast. What time do you reckon your man will be able to get here?"

"Farmers work early. I'll give him a ring at six and see what he says. So long as that door stays shut it don't much matter what time he comes over. Just make sure George doesn't come out and open it up."

"I will, you can be sure of that. Oh, Stevie! You are a wonder! What a stroke of luck!"

They embraced again and then stood close to the garage door, listening intently. Was that the sound of some movement inside? The big black greyhound was trapped! Got it! Annabel was hugging herself in triumph. No more nightmares!

The two kissed quickly and went their respective ways to their respective houses. Annabel took one last triumphant look out of the bedroom window before getting into bed and drawing up the covers around her neck. She was ecstatic.

* * *

Still trying to get comfortable in his makeshift bed, Greyhound George jumped as the garage door behind him was suddenly slammed shut.

Oh ho! he thought. *Someone has seen me entering the garage and has now locked me in.* Except the door couldn't be locked. He had the only key. *Still, I'm stuck*, he thought. There was no way he could squeeze around the back of the Land Rover to the garage door and twist the handle that released the catch. The locking mechanism engaged on all four sides of the door: top, bottom and both sides. Easy enough to twist round and release it if you had hands, but not at all possible in your mouth, especially squashed sideways between the door and the Land Rover.

What are they up to? His head was a little foggy still after all the night's drinking but, in trying to put his thoughts in order, he could remember Smarmy Stephen waiting for him one time with a cricket bat to knock his brains out. Maybe he was trying again? George got up and padded to the door and listened carefully. Could he hear anything?

There were voices out there talking excitedly. It was Smarmy Stephen and Annabel, he was sure of it – who else would it be? But he couldn't catch what they were saying. Whatever it was, George reckoned, it wasn't going to be good for his health. After all, Smarmy Stephen wanted to strangle or skewer Mr Tibbs with a garden fork and that cat had done nothing but shit in the Maxwell garden on the odd occasion. George had committed far more serious crimes. He'd tried to wake up the neighbourhood with his barking; wrecked Smarmy Stephen's flower beds; run in and out of his house; chased and terrified his mistress. That must qualify George for some serious redesign of his canine anatomy if they could ever catch him. And now they had. Hmmm.

George looked about the garage. There was some lamplight that shone in through a small window high up and, although his head ached, he could just make out the time on the clock he kept on the work bench. It was a little after one in the morning. Well it was unlikely his wife and her lover would pull any stunt just yet. They would most likely go to bed and come and see him in the morning – if he was still here. George decided his best strategy was to go to sleep himself and see if he could work any changes in the night. There was nothing else to do, after all.

George settled down for the second time on his foam rubber and overcoat. His head was telling him in no uncertain fashion to close his eyes and close his thoughts. He readily obliged.

It was the sound of an insistent beep-beeping as some vehicle or other was reversing close by that next registered in George's brain. His eyes flickered open and he tried to come round, notwithstanding the fog that seemed to be obstructing his vision. Where was he? What time was it? George was still hung-over and had just struggled to his feet when then there was a sudden, sharp *bang* and light flooded the interior of the garage. The garage! He was in the garage. And the door had just flown up.

"George!" A cry of surprise. "What are you doing here?"

George was busy dusting himself down and smiling to himself at his returned human form when he was confronted by Smarmy Stephen. On the other side of the garage, shuffling along between the Land Rover and the far wall, another man was entering that George didn't recognise at all.

"Hello, Stephen. What are *you* doing here?" He looked at both men, one then the other. "And what are you two up to in my garage? Trying to steal my motor?"

"Er, no…we're looking for something…a dog…"

"Of course. In my garage. Do you think I keep one in my Land Rover? Or was it one of those robotic, motorised dogs you were looking for this time? Maybe you thought I'd parked one in here?"

"No, no…it's an ordinary dog we want."

"Last time it was in my garden. Now in my garage. Next time in my house? What is it about you and dogs, Stephen? Can't you think of somewhere else to look for them? Why not your own property for a change?" George was enjoying this. Stephen Maxwell could hardly confess to his intimacy with George's wife and all her demands.

As Smarmy Stephen squirmed, George glanced across at the other man who had now slid along to the front of the Land Rover and was looking like a spare part in an amateur dramatic production. He was standing idly, his hands behind his back, hoping he wouldn't be noticed. A trifle difficult in the confined space the three men occupied.

"Who's your friend?" George asked.

"Oh, er, just a friend of mine…"

"Well, shall we go out then and make introductions outside? Maybe you can find your dog there."

Smarmy Stephen had no option but to turn and sidle his way out. George stood his ground and indicated that the other man should do the same. Then he followed on and moved after them. As he got outside, he noticed Smarmy Stephen had ducked down and was peering under the Land Rover.

"Nothing there but a bit of spilt oil and water, Stephen. Did you want to crawl under and check? Oh, hello, Annabel. What are you doing here? Want to go for a ride?"

"George! What were you doing in there?" She was looking absolutely furious.

"Well I wasn't looking for any dog, nor was I going to drive the Land Rover out." George peered down at himself, still dressed in his now somewhat crumpled dinner jacket and full regalia. "Nor was I entertaining friends for dinner in my motor. But what were you three trying to get into my garage for?" He looked at the rear of a large Transit van that was now backed up, with its double doors gaping wide just a few feet away from the open garage. "Or were you going to load up this wagon with something?" He looked at Annabel, Smarmy Stephen and the spare-part man – most likely the van driver, George thought.

Not one of the three wanted to say anything. They all looked as guilty as sin. The van driver was holding something black and ominous and evil in one hand behind his back.

Annabel couldn't hold her frustration in any longer. "George, did you let that black monster out?"

"I don't keep any monsters hidden in the garage, Annabel. Nor do I hide them under the beds. And the last I saw, there were no dragons flying around Durham Castle either. I would have thought you'd have grown out of those nightmares by now"

"I hate it when you're being facetious, George. I'm talking about that dog. That big, vicious, greyhound that causes so much trouble. Did you let it out of the garage in the night? You must have done and you know it. Why else were you in there?"

"It may surprise you, Annabel, but I do not go around looking to release all the dogs in hell to go chase after you…" As George was saying this the van driver was trying to creep away unnoticed to the front of his vehicle, carrying that ugly something that looked a little like a black, cumbersome electric drill. A little. Only it seemed to be more like a sort of gun.

George stopped. He looked again at the man, anxious to get away, climbing into his van and trying to conceal his gun. He looked at the two others: his wife with a face of anger and frustration and Smarmy Stephen – slippery, evasive and smarmy as always. He suddenly realised, with horror, that these three had been on their way to kill him.

"Why, you bloodthirsty murderers! You were looking to kill

that dog, weren't you!" George realised he had escaped death only by the good fortune of metamorphosing in his sleep. "What gives you the right to take out your venom on poor, defenceless animals? Just because you don't like dogs, Annabel, so you want to go and murder them! Who's the vicious monster now? Eh?"

"Don't be so melodramatic, George!" Annabel gave vent to all the frustration that her husband had caused her, depriving her of the solution to her nightmares. "That's a stray dog. A public nuisance. We're doing everyone a favour – the council put down stray dogs all the time."

"How do you know he's a stray? He was nuisance for you, no one else. That's all the excuse you need to kill him? God help any other creature you don't like!" George span round and slammed shut the rear doors of the Transit van. "Go on! Clear off!" he shouted at the driver. Then he turned to Smarmy Stephen. He was angry.

"You'd better go home too, Stephen. And don't go poking around in my garage or my back garden again – with cricket bats, or so-called friends, or whatever!" George stormed off through the back garden and into the house. He couldn't look at his wife.

George went upstairs, stripped off his hired outfit and took a shower. Standing under the stream of water helped cool his temper and allowed him to think. He made his mind up. Decisions were taken. Things had to change and he wasn't going to continue living the farce his marriage had become for any longer. George towelled himself off, changed and, with the dress uniform now folded and packed up, he went downstairs for breakfast and to confront his wife.

"Annabel, I've got to go into Durham this morning to take this outfit back where I got it from, and after that I'll go see the lawyers. You and I will get a divorce."

Annabel did her best to imitate a volcano erupting but it didn't fool George in the slightest.

"Come off it, Annabel! You know that's what you want. You

can then go and move in with Smarmy Stephen – you're in there more often than here these days, so I'm told. Then I'll put this house up for sale. Come to think of it, after the lawyers, I'll go visit the estate agents and have them come and value the place. It should fetch quite a tidy sum after all these years."

Volcano simulations were redoubled with the use of various cushions and soft furnishings playing the role of molten lava flying to all parts.

"Very impressive, Annabel. You're just annoyed that I've made the decision and not you. Whilst I'm out, do make a start in packing things up and moving what you want to Stephen's house. Take anything and everything you want, except for what's in my study. Oh – and just in case of any reluctance on your part to move out, I'll go looking for that dog to bring back with me to live here. He and I will be sure to get on well together in your absence."

This was pure bluff on his part, as George well knew, but his last attempt at such poker play had come off rather well so he thought he'd try it again. Annabel meanwhile had graduated from pyroclastic displays to major tectonic earth movements. George reckoned it was time for a quick exit. Breakfast, he thought, would be a trifle difficult to organise in the sulphurous atmosphere he had just helped create so he'd go without and eat in town somewhere. He turned to leave the house and to leave Annabel to do whatever she damn well wanted to do – hoping that it was not to bury a carving knife between his shoulder blades as he reached for the back door. That would make driving into town a little difficult.

George made it to the back gate without mishap. He quickly went through and shut it behind him – and then found himself doing a little jig in the lane outside his garage. He'd done it! Liberation at last! After over twenty years of marriage there would no doubt be all sorts of legal hoops to jump through to finally secure the divorce and, knowing Annabel, she would fight to get as much out of him as possible. It would probably cost him more than a pound of flesh to rid himself of her – but he didn't care now. The decision had been made.

George was whistling as he opened the garage door, backed out his Land Rover and prepared to depart for Durham. Maybe he'd give the girls a ring and drop in to see them when he'd finished business in town. He felt he owed Carol an apology for doggifying in front of her last night. He still felt guilty about that.

George climbed down from his motor, shut and locked the garage door, then got back up behind the wheel and put the Land Rover into gear. Maybe he'd offer to take Rosie for run? Maybe he'd take his motor off-road somewhere? Maybe he'd disappear into the wild blue yonder and never come back? Anything and everything was possible now. George put his foot down and drove off. He was a happy man.

It was a couple of hours later when the Land Rover drew up outside the girls' house. He parked behind a long grey Volvo, Duncan's car. George hadn't phoned; his head was too full of the information and the ideas his recent meetings had given him. It turned out that the divorce was not going to be so difficult after all – with no kids, both employed with not dissimilar incomes and George likely to have more evidence to show he was the aggrieved party; it ought not to involve a long-drawn-out fight for freedom. George reckoned that when Annabel calmed down she would readily agree to end it all, providing she would get at least half the value of the house. He'd go along with that just to get rid of her.

George rang the bell on the girls' front door; he was still whistling happily to himself, full of the joys of this late spring. No answer. He rang again. There was still no answer so he bent down and hollered through the letter box: "Anyone in?"

A window opened suddenly above him and the naked half of

Duncan appeared, his hair dishevelled and sticking out at all angles.

"Hello there, Duncan," George called up cheerily. "And how's life treating you this fine morning?"

The head went back in and called out to someone behind: "It's George!" Then he leaned out again and looked down. "Och, man, life will be treating me a whole lot better when I get this wild cat off my back!"

There was a screech behind and a pillow was pounded on the Scotsman's head, rearranging his hairstyle again. Duncan withdrew. There was then a certain amount of scrabbling that could be heard and finally Sally's top half emerged wrapped in a towel. She tried to speak but was clearly battling to stay in one place by the window. Then her towel disappeared and Sally squawked, disappearing rapidly after it. A moment's delay and her head, only her head, showed above.

"Hello, George," she cried out, "I can't let you in just yet but if you're looking for Carol, she went out with Rosie twenty minutes ago..."

"Any idea where?"

"Yes..." came a strangled reply. "If you drive up to the end of the next road...Gerroff!...and then hop across the pedestrian footbridge over the railway...there's the footpath there where you ought to be able to cut her off..." Sally's head was pulled away and Duncan's reappeared.

"Good luck, mon. Give her one for me!"

"Thank you, Duncan. I'll endeavour to do that." George could see that any further conversation was not likely to be fruitful. He left them to it.

George clambered up the steps of the footbridge and followed it across to green fields that spread out on the other side. A footpath ran away from him, leading into a patch of woodland some distance away. He could see no one as yet so he picked up his pace across the grass, taking care not to get himself too muddy in the process. He looked across the field. This one and the next seemed to contain four or five horses. Nothing else; no dog walkers as yet.

George was wondering how he would find Carol and what he was going to say to her when he did, and then Rosie came catapulting towards him from out of the woods. George stopped and let her jump and run all round him. She was clearly happy to see him and so was George to meet her. He was a little nervous about seeing her owner, however.

"Hello, George. Back with us again?" Carol looked at him coolly.

"Yes. I wanted to come and see you."

"How long for this time?"

George blushed. "I'm sorry. I don't do it on purpose. It just sort of happens…"

Carol stopped in front of him. She was still upset. "Don't tell me that, George. You must have some kind of idea of what you are doing. Isn't it about time you sorted yourself out?"

"Yes. You're right. That's what I wanted to see you for." George looked at her. She was wearing her tracksuit again, just the same as the first time he'd seen her and she was just as delicious. But the atmosphere between them this time was completely different. Her lively teasing of him and his whole lifestyle could not continue any longer. The canine transformations had been fun at first but she had wanted more from him last night and he'd turned away from her again rather than respond. That hurt. Things couldn't go on like this.

"Well…you're seeing me now." The tone of voice was flat. Her green eyes were looking at him, expressionless, waiting. Carol was not giving an inch.

For a moment, George didn't know what to say. There was an awkward silence. Then he gave a grin. She had always had a profoundly unsettling effect upon him that stirred up his feelings no end but this time he had just come back from an exceedingly productive set of meetings and he suddenly felt as free as a greyhound – although now in his customary, albeit somewhat depreciated human frame. He actually felt like barking.

"Thank you!" he suddenly blurted out. To Carol's surprise he grabbed both of her hands and whirled her around in rather an uncoordinated pirouette. "Thankyou, thankyou, thankyou!" He kept grinning and parroting the same sentiment like a cracked record.

"George! What's got into you?" Carol tried not to smile.

George stopped, a bit puffed. He was no athlete after all, not in this guise anyway. "I don't know what brought you into my world, you and Rosie together, and for the life of me I don't know what you are still doing in it...but thanks to you my world is going to be the same no longer. I've just filed for a divorce!"

"*No!* Well congratulations, George, but why thank me? It was going to happen anyway, wasn't it?"

"Maybe not...I might have struggled on for years more – quietly suffering, wasting away. Who knows in what state I would have ended up? But not now, not since I met you and Rosie; not since I started doggifying. I started to see the whole world from an entirely different perspective. It was all due to you, and of course Rosie."

The said dog came up and nuzzled George who enthusiastically stroked and fussed over her. He bent down to receive a lick on his nose and, although not able to converse fluently in animal-speak in his present configuration, he did his best to tell her what a good dog, what a magical dog she was and how indebted he was to her.

Carol stood back and waited. "When you two have quite finished your love affair, do you think we can resume our walk now?" She felt a bit peeved, a bit superfluous.

George stood back up. "No. I haven't finished with you yet. I have to talk to you. You know it's *you* that makes me jump out of my skin, don't you? I mean its Rosie and her breed that I end up resembling…but it's you that's doing it. That and I guess a certain intake of alcohol that seems to lubricate the process and flick the trigger, so to speak…"

Carol just looked at him. Those gorgeous green eyes were doing it again. George began to feel hot under the collar, his pulse began to speed up. *Goddammit*, he thought, *I can't lose it again! Not now, not here!* He had to look away and take a few deep breaths.

"Carol!" He span round. "Why do you bother with me? You looked absolutely ravishing last night and there was any number of blokes in the SCR just dying to get to know you but you stuck next to me all the time, an ugly, decaying, middle-aged old fossil, and you didn't give anyone else a look in. Why not? They're all better-looking, better paid, better clued-up than I am. What are you doing with me?"

Carol grinned. "Maybe I'm fed up with all those young, narcissistic types? Maybe it's time I had a fling with an old fossil or two? Actually, you looked fantastic last night. Really distinguished. Actually quite good-looking. You scrub up well for an old fossil, you know. Did you know that, George?" She was teasing him now. That was good.

"Look, you stupid, glorious, phenomenally sexy young filly…I've been trying my very best for weeks not to look at you and go all weak at the knees. You're what, twenty-seven, twenty-eight? I'm fifty-five. Decades older than you! What are you doing hanging around me, unless you get a sadistic thrill torturing old geezers like I am?"

Carol's smile widened further and she put her arms up around his neck. "That's right. I regularly do this. See how many old men I can make keel over. Give 'em heart attacks. Polish them off. Save the National Health Service a fortune in old-age care…"

"You wicked, evil, murderous young woman. You ought to be locked up!" Carol's face was inches from George's own. He couldn't resist it any longer. He kissed her. Then he went all wobbly and began to fall.

"George!" Carol held onto him in alarm. They both staggered and plunged about on the uneven surface of the footpath. Even Rosie bounded back in surprise, until George righted himself and stood back up, straight and erect.

"Well, that's what you want isn't it? Knock me over? Do away with me so you can move on to the next one?"

"George that was not funny!"

"I thought it was. Actually, that's what you can expect, isn't it, fooling around with old geriatrics like me. What do you think you are doing? I've asked you already and I want an answer – why are you bothering with me?"

"And I've already told you before. I love you to bits!"

"You must be crazy. You can't really mean it. I'm old enough to be your father."

"Not quite. He would have been a few years your senior, had he lived. I lost him a long time ago, when I was little girl. That's what I'm looking for, of course. A father substitute."

George struggled to remove her arms from around his neck. "Oh no! I'm not having that!"

Carol fought to hang on. "George, I didn't mean it. I didn't! I didn't!" She kissed him frantically, despite him trying to wriggle away.

George stopped and looked at her for the umpteenth time. "You're a beautiful girl. Be serious. You can't really want to have me for a partner. Can you?"

Carol looked back. She nodded.

"Am I just a passing fancy, a quick fling with an older bloke for a change, or are you serious? Be careful what you say now."

"George, I want you. I want your babies. I want you to fill me up with babies! Understand? Is that serious enough for you? In fact, why don't we start right now? Come back into the woods this instant. If you're so geriatric, like you say you are, I'd better get as many babies out of you as I can before you keel over and I lose you. OK?"

"Good God!"

"George, how many more times do I have to tell you? I love you. What about you? How do you feel about me?"

"I've been trying to stop myself falling in love with you ever since I first saw you. Why do I end up turning into a greyhound? It seems to be the only way I can stop myself making a complete fool of myself, the only way I can resist you. Even then it's not easy…"

"Well stop trying to stop yourself. Got that? Just give the girl what she wants. A little bit of love and affection." Carol put her arms back around him and kissed him again. Gently. This time George didn't try to wriggle away.

Chapter 16

George drove Carol and Rosie the short distance two streets back to their home and parked outside. Duncan's Volvo had gone. Carol opened up and checked inside – as she guessed, Sally was out: Duncan and she were most likely on their way to his place in Newcastle.

Rosie wandered into the kitchen, snaffled up a little of the dog food that Carol had put down for her earlier and then retired to the front room and climbed up onto the sofa. George knew only too well how she felt – after her run out, then something to eat, it was now time to lie down and have a rest. Greyhounds, like all active carnivores who burn up a lot of energy, spend a lot of time sleeping.

That left George and Carol on their own, looking at one another.

"Did you really mean what you said about wanting babies?" George asked, hopefully.

Carol grinned. "Absolutely. If I'm not fertile right away, we can certainly try practising..."

There was a sudden stampede for the bedroom upstairs and the next hour was spent in unrestrained debauchery.

George fell back almost exhausted. "You are going to kill me sooner rather than later, did you know that?"

"You'll die happy though, won't you?"

"I can't think of a better way to go." George turned round to gaze into Carol's face. There was a serenity, a gentleness there, that captured his heart. She was so lovely he felt he might burst.

"I've never wanted kids before, do you know that? I've never really wanted to think about it because deep down, all along, I've known why not. I've never wanted kids with *her*."

"And now?"

George leapt upon Carol. She giggled and squirmed delightfully. He growled: "Like you said – I want to fill you up with 'em. Babies, babies and more babies!"

Twenty gymnastic minutes passed and this time George *was* exhausted. He could barely move. Carol kissed the back of his neck while he lay spread-eagled beside her.

"You're a bit of a tiger, d'you know that? Not so much a greyhound. Not so much an old man. I was right all along, wasn't I? There's a wildness in you that's been there for ages and ages and that needs to be let out."

"Mmm. No wildness left. All gone," George mumbled. "You've done for me. Death awaits. Sadist!"

Carol laughed. In contrast to the man beside her, she was invigorated. "You'll live. You haven't eaten today have you? I'll go and fix lunch." She got up and disappeared downstairs.

It was late afternoon when George eventually drove his Land Rover back into the garage and parked it there. He drew down the door and locked it. He knew intuitively that he wouldn't need to leave it open for his greyhound alter ego to enter. He had a feeling that his canine transformation episodes were over. His life had unalterably changed; there was no need for his body to do so.

George was a new man. He stepped with springs in his heels into the back garden and there, to his delight, was Mr Tibbs waiting to welcome him – an auspicious sign if ever there was one.

"Hello, Tibbs, you old scoundrel. What are you doing here?" George was hoping it meant what he thought it meant. He let himself in by the back door and looked around. The place was empty. No Annabel.

"Come in and have a look round, Tibbs," he called out. "You're very welcome!"

George's furry friend and accomplice took no second bidding. In he strolled as if he owned the place and proceeded to inspect the various rooms. George did the same – checking what had been taken and what was left behind. As it turned out, Annabel had taken most of her own belongings and a fair amount of movables from the kitchen and bathroom but nothing much else. Their joint possessions – all the heavy stuff – would have to be divided up later, George understood, but he wasn't much bothered with that. So long as his wife had gone. He went into the study, took out his whisky flask and then repaired to the lounge where he spread himself out in the armchair and took stock of all that had happened.

He was so relaxed now he was almost comatose. The men from the estate agents would come on Monday morning and put a 'For Sale' notice up in front. George would have to see Annabel (groan!) to sort out what she wanted and what he could take. Maybe he would rent somewhere to live for the time being? Maybe he could put stuff from the house in storage and leave it empty as soon as possible to show to prospective buyers? All sorts of decisions would have to be taken soon but for the moment he could just lie here with a stupid grin on his face. This evening he had asked Carol to come out with him – an earlier promise that now took on an entirely different meaning. They'd maybe go to a pub or restaurant so that they could talk and decide what to do. In his case he knew exactly what he wanted – to move in with her straight away – but he'd have to wait and see what her plans were first.

George tipped up the flask and sampled just the slightest sip of 10-year-old Ardbeg. No need to slosh it back; he just wanted a taste, the merest tiny reprise of all the adventures he had been through in the last month or so. How things change. He could not stop smirking at life's vicissitudes and where it had left him. He was dog-tired, of course. Well, man-tired. He had slept in a garage, badly and not for very long last night. He had indulged in an extremely exhausting but unbelievably sexually satisfying afternoon. And now he was in an empty house, with a neighbour's cat and his brain was full of images of a beautiful young woman that he had recently left behind and who would be waiting for him in a couple of hours' time. Could life get any better? He fell asleep with the savour of single malt whisky in his mouth.

It was eight o'clock in the evening when George next came round. The first thing he did was look down and check himself. Thank goodness! He didn't think that Carol would be too pleased if he turned up as a black greyhound again, no matter how elegant and well-turned-out an animal he could be in his alternate lifestyle. There was a moment's regret. He had really enjoyed the liberation that his canine other self had given him. No more charging around and playing the anarchic influence on any number of unsuspecting folk; no more crazy runs through dining halls, roads, fields and wherever his fancy took him. He had to return to being the respectable, middle-aged pillar of society that he had spent a lifetime creating. Shame! George supposed he could afford a minute or two's commiseration over the loss of rejuvenation that he had enjoyed. Well, no need to linger over it. That short-lived period of transformation had achieved what was necessary. His mid-life crisis was over. The next phase in his life was about to begin…and there was to be no more doggification.

George drove Carol up to Palace Green and parked right in front of Durham Cathedral. The summer sun was low but it was still bright, throwing long shadows across the green. This was a magical place, a romantic place, no matter it was at the heart of the University of Durham where various colleges and the sense of academe stretched all around you. George had sampled a fair slice of that society recently and was no longer in awe of it. He also had a very special member of the university staff at his elbow and if she was the representative of the finer side of that institution, he couldn't get enough of it. His intimate knowledge of a certain other female employee of the university had, up until now, always made him want to run as far as possible in the other direction.

There was a noise that interrupted George's meditation that came to him from the grounds of the cathedral, from behind the low wall that contained a number of old tombstones. It was the sound of dogs running around and barking.

George grimaced at Carol. "I can't help it," he said. "I've just got to go see what all the bother is about. They might be friends of mine!"

Carol looked heavenwards. "Good grief! Is that what living with you is going to be like now? Investigating every pooch that crosses your path?"

George didn't answer. He was already on his way. He called out and almost immediately four dogs veered in his direction. He recognised them! It was Rufus, Mucker and a couple of heavy-jowled friends he'd not seen before. It was the Durham Pack of strays, wastrels and reprobates. George was delighted.

Carol stood back a little to watch the little gathering. There was no way she wanted all sorts of stray dogs jumping up and drooling all over her. There was no such reserve displayed by her partner however, who it must be said, did not suffer any such antics either. His doggy friends were suitably reverential. George was clearly the leader of the pack and although they all obviously enjoyed each other's company there was no indiscipline about their communal behaviour.

Carol gave it a minute or two, then commented drily, "Is this your idea of taking a girl out for the evening? Going to the dogs? C'mon, George, I didn't get all dressed up this evening to watch you run about with a pack of hounds!"

George got the message. "Sorry, beautiful, but I only paused to say hello. To see if they recognised me. It was Rufus and Mucker with some mates of theirs. You remember them? They took part in the dog display that upended your geophysics friend a week back."

"Yes, yes, I'm sure you're all delighted to see each other again. Is that how it's going to be every time we go out, George? Or worse, are you going to have them all come and visit us at home?"

George stopped, put his arm around Carol's waist and drew her to him. "Are we going to make home together then?" he asked pointedly.

"Only if we have *one* dog with us. Rosie. I don't want half the dogs in Durham wandering in and out."

George gave her a kiss. "Done. Where are we going to live?"

"I don't want to get into that here. Where are you taking me? Let's go in somewhere and talk about this over a drink or something."

George led the way down from Palace Green past the market place towards the River Wear. Saturday night in Durham city centre was crowded but George had booked a table at a riverside Italian restaurant where there was less of a crowd and they had time to stretch out, talk and investigate each other's ideas of what future lay in front of them. It was a brilliant evening, with much laughter and teasing, one of the other. There was one worrying issue, however, that eventually raised its head and that Carol was anxious to dispel.

"George, I'm not going to wake up beside you one night and find a dog next to me, am I? I mean, I love you in all your idiosyncratic ways…but much as I love greyhounds, I don't want to snuggle up with one."

"No love. I think my dog days are over. If you marry me now I don't think I'll ever metamorphose again."

"Is that a marriage proposal, or blackmail?"

George leant across the spaghetti and kissed her. "It's a marriage proposal. When I'm able to, will you have me?"

Carol looked him up and down. She grinned. She paused for dramatic effect. "Dunno!"

"Bitch!"

Carol leapt across and threw her arms about him, laughing crazily. People on the surrounding tables stopped eating. "I was hoping I could join you one day like that! You a dog and me a bitch. Whaddya say? Shall we try? It would be absolutely *beastly*!"

George struggled to free himself and nodded to the other tables around in apology. "My niece," he explained. "Do excuse her. A very emotional character!"

Carol was by now standing over him. She raised her voice: "Liar! George – don't you dare try that ever again!" She looked around at the other tables and nodded in apology. "I'm his, um, escort. He's my client. He pays very well…"

George started fizzing. He was red in the face and his temperature had soared but there was no canine transformation that was going to get him out of this.

"I've told you. No more greyhounds. Not me, nor you, so please sit down and stop making a scene. And marry me!"

Carol was still laughing. "I will, George. I will. As soon as possible. OK? Now come home with me and take me to bed again."

The waiter was summoned, the bill paid and the two of them gathered their bits together and made to leave. Carol was hanging on to George's arm as they ventured outside. It was dark now as they crossed the river on their way towards Palace Green and the waiting Land Rover.

It was not quite pub turning-out time yet but still there were numbers of people moving up and down the lane leading from the market place. George and Carol stood aside by the bridge for a moment to avoid the crush.

Suddenly, a big man appeared. He pushed George violently against the stone wall behind and ripped Carol's handbag out of her grasp. He then turned to run down the towpath beside the river, giving George a kick as he stepped over him.

"Out of the way, you bastard, or I'll break your leg. Leave the lady's things to me."

Carol screamed but the man was gone, vanishing at top speed into the darkness where no lights shone beyond the bridge.

George rolled over. He felt a jolt of electricity surging through his veins. Without thinking, he was up and running, accelerating at a furious pace giving full vent to his feelings. He was sure that half of Durham could hear him barking and snarling like he had never done before. He was furious and he flew. Soft earth from the towpath cascaded up behind him as his feet pounded along ever faster. The stretch of river here was dark but dead straight and there was no contest in the race. The thug could not have got more than twenty yards when, despite a delayed start, a large black greyhound came out of nowhere to sink his teeth into his forearm and drag him down.

"Aarg! Get the fuck off me, you fiend!" He was a big brute of a man, down on one knee with his lower arm being wrenched and torn by the greyhound, but the dog was not heavy enough to immobilise the thief. He struck out with his other hand to try and dislodge George.

Then four other dogs came baying at full pelt down the towpath: the Durham Pack of strays, wastrels and reprobates. They piled straight into the big man with no delay, who buckled and tipped over. George found himself on top of the man staring straight into his eyes.

Greyhounds have vicious-looking teeth, equipped to slash and tear their quarry. George drew his lips back and let the man have full view of his double set of weaponry whilst his friends took hold of his arms and legs. He told his captive that his thieving behaviour was not appreciated. Not appreciated at all, did he understand? In fact if he was ever to show his face again on Durham riverside he might not have a face left next time. Was he in any doubt about what he was being told? George moved with inches of the man's throat just as so as to make things crystal clear. He told him: *Now do run along, old scout; leave ladies' handbags alone, and don't come back, OK?*

Once the man had got the message, George climbed off him. His four friends relented also. They watched the one-time thug stagger away, now scratched, bleeding and with at least one arm mangled and looking like a reject from a butcher's shop.

George was quite eloquent in his thanks of his four friends. They on their part were only too pleased to help with an honoured member of the Durham Pack who Rufus and Mucker had spoken most admiringly of in the past. George touched noses with all and said he must be going now – it wasn't right to keep a lady waiting. His buddies all understood. They said cheerio and hoped that they could all meet up another time. Wasn't this fun, after all? With that they trotted off away up the towpath.

Carol was left stranded on the bridge, gasping at what had just happened. And here came George, grinning ruefully out of the darkness and holding up her handbag that had just been stolen from her grasp.

"George…" She was flabbergasted. She didn't know what to say and could only burst into tears. George took hold of her.

"I know. Frightening. A terrible shock. He was brute of a man."

"But, George, I looked round and you…you were a *greyhound!*"

"Yes. I know. Don't ask how – it just happened. And just as well it did."

"But…but you said your dog days are over."

"I thought they were. Come on, let's go home."

Later that night, warm and wrapped around one another in bed, exhausted again after another hour or so of lovemaking, Carol nuzzled George's ear.

"George…" she whispered.

"Mmm?"

"You're not going to doggify in the night are you?"

"Nope."

Carol raised herself on one elbow and peered intently at him.

"How do you know? Just tell me that, will you! You said it wasn't going to happen ever again."

"I know."

George looked down at her. This time the glorious golden globes were pressed warm and tender up against his chest and he was the happiest man in the universe and had absolutely no desire whatever to metamorphose into any other creature.

"With you, gorgeous, I'll never run away from your embraces again. I'll never again have to tear my eyes away from you; to resort to dogginess. I can relax and get control of my life at last. But...it turns out..."

"What?"

"It turns out, I think, that if necessary...if absolutely necessary...if my decrepit old frame isn't up to defending you like I should...well then, I can become Greyhound George again. It seems...after all this... that *I can switch it on and off!*"

"Why, you old dog!"

"Yes. Life from now on is certainly going to be interesting..."

At Roundfire we publish great stories. We lean towards the spiritual and thought-provoking. But whether it's literary or popular, a gentle tale or a pulsating thriller, the connecting theme in all Roundfire fiction titles is that once you pick them up you won't want to put them down.